The Case of the Quizzical Queens Beagle

A Thousand Islands Doggy Inn Mystery

B.R. Snow

Copyright © 2018 B.R. Snow

ISBN: 978-1-942691-46-4

Website: www.brsnow.net/
Twitter: @BernSnow
Facebook: facebook.com/bernsnow

Cover Design: Reggie Cullen

Cover Photo: James R. Miller

Other Books by B.R. Snow

The Thousand Islands Doggy Inn Mysteries

- The Case of the Abandoned Aussie
- The Case of the Brokenhearted Bulldog
- The Case of the Caged Cockers
- The Case of the Dapper Dandie Dinmont
- The Case of the Eccentric Elkhound
- The Case of the Faithful Frenchie
- The Case of the Graceful Goldens
- The Case of the Hurricane Hounds
- The Case of the Itinerant Ibizan
- The Case of the Jaded Jack Russell
- The Case of the Klutz King Charles
- The Case of the Lovable Labs
- The Case of the Mellow Maltese
- The Case of the Natty Newfie
- The Case of the Overdue Otterhound
- The Case of the Prescient Poodle

The Whiskey Run Chronicles

- Episode 1 – The Dry Season Approaches
- Episode 2 – Friends and Enemies
- Episode 3 – Let the Games Begin
- Episode 4 – Enter the Revenuer
- Episode 5 – A Changing Landscape
- Episode 6 – Entrepreneurial Spirits
- Episode 7 – All Hands On Deck
- The Whiskey Run Chronicles – The Complete Volume 1

The Damaged Posse

- American Midnight
- Larrikin Gene
- Sneaker World
- Summerman
- The Duplicates

Other Books

- Divorce Hotel
- Either Ore

To Laurie and Stella

Chapter 1

I gently slid the smallmouth bass back into the water and watched it disappear with a flick of its tail. I rinsed my hands in the still-not-warm-enough-to-get-in water then dried them with a towel and leaned my fishing pole against the seat.

"I think I've had enough," I said, refilling both our coffees.

"Me too," Josie said, reeling her line in. "So, you're saying you've finally calmed down?"

"For the moment," I said, stretching out on the seat. "And if I can manage to avoid seeing her today, I should be able to stay that way."

Josie chuckled as she placed her pole next to mine.

"Look at this way, marriage is going to be a piece of cake after you guys get through this," she said, sipping her coffee. "And your mom just wants your wedding to be perfect."

"Where exactly does an eight-foot ice sculpture of the bride and groom fit into your definition of perfect?" I said, raising an eyebrow at her.

"Yeah, I didn't see that one coming," Josie said, laughing. "But it will be August. Maybe it'll be really hot that day, and it'll melt fast."

"At this rate, I'm never going to make it to August."

"Hey, you're inside a hundred days," she said, digging through the cooler to retrieve a container packed with pastries. "It's the homestretch."

I grabbed a blueberry muffin and quickly worked my way through it as I looked out at the calm water bathed in early morning light.

"Three more months," I said, shaking my head. "I wonder what she's going to come up with next."

"Just try to roll with it," Josie said. "The more you argue with her, the more she digs in."

"Whose wedding does she think it is?"

"Oh, it's way too early in the morning for rhetorical. Just eat your muffin."

We'd made the decision to go fishing last night after I'd gone another ten rounds with my mother about her latest additions to my wedding day. At first, our conversation had gone well, the eight-foot ice sculpture notwithstanding, but had gone downhill after she, again, brought up the guest list for additional discussion and debate. And her decision to invite a couple I barely knew had opened the floodgates. Unwilling to run the risk of offending anyone, she had quickly added another forty people to the invitee list and crossed the five hundred mark. And given that the guest list had been expanded, a two-hour conversation about the required changes to the seating arrangements ensued that left my mother exasperated with her *belligerent moppet* and me exhausted and grumpy and threatening a Vegas elopement.

It was at that point when Josie had suggested a morning of fishing on the River sans my mom.

I reached for one of the rapidly disappearing chocolate crullers then spotted a bizarre and brightly colored vessel heading downriver in the main channel several hundred yards away.

"What the heck is that?" I said.

"I have no idea," Josie said, reaching for a pair of binoculars. "It's not big enough to be a commercial ship." She focused the glasses on the boat then handed them to me. "A circus? That's weird."

Using the binoculars, I scanned the boat from bow to stern. It had to be a couple hundred feet long and sat about ten feet above the water. Painted yellow and purple with red accents, the sign on the side displayed the name *Pontilly Family Circus* in cursive script. I lowered the glasses and handed them back to Josie who took another look before tossing them on the seat next to her.

"A circus that travels by boat?" I said, frowning. "Have you ever heard of anything like that?"

"Never," she said, shaking her head. "The cages on the deck tell me they have animal acts. And you know how we both feel about those."

"Yeah," I said, reaching for the binoculars and taking another look. Then I scowled. "Great. Somebody onboard just tossed something in the water."

"What was it?"

"I'm not sure, but it looked like a bag of garbage," I said, setting the glasses down. "Unbelievable."

Both of us deplored circuses with wild animals acts as well as the barbaric methods used to train them. And we'd been delighted when many countries began banning circuses using those acts from performing. But for reasons inexplicable to us, both Canada and the States continued to allow them apart from some jurisdictions that had seen the light and instituted local bans.

And we hated people throwing crap in the River just as much.

"How's your morning schedule?" I said.

"It's clear until eleven," she said, cutting the last cruller in half. "It's such a beautiful morning. You want to hang out here?"

"Why don't we just cruise around awhile?" I said.

"Sounds great. We should have brought the dogs."

"They have a way of ruining the fishing," I said. "There's no way we could keep them out of the water on a day like this."

"Not to mention us being able to stay dry," she said, stretching out and putting her feet up on the seat.

I started the engine, and we headed upriver away from the main channel and spent the next hour working our way through the islands. We briefly entered Canadian waters, then turned around and headed for home. I slowed when we reached the main channel and waited for a large ship to pass. It had to be at least 700 feet long and was heading upriver toward Lake Ontario. We watched until it disappeared from sight, then I accelerated and crossed the channel at a forty-five-degree angle that would take us directly to the Inn.

I waved to a passing boater then glanced over at Josie when she nudged my arm. I followed her eyes and slowed to an idle.

"Is that what I think it is?" I said, staring at the buoy about a hundred feet in front of us.

"Oh, good. You see it, too. For a second there, I thought you might have put something in the muffins."

The buoy in question was one of the markers used during the Seaway season to designate the outer edge of the deep-water channel ships used to navigate through a potentially treacherous section of the River dotted with islands of all shapes and sizes. It was painted green, about ten feet wide with a small platform that sat about three feet above the waterline. But it wasn't the buoy itself that had us staring in disbelief. It was the small dog standing on it and staring back with its head cocked that left us with our mouths open.

"Toy beagle, right?" Josie said.

"Yeah, what a gorgeous dog," I said, slowly approaching the buoy. "How the heck did it get up there?"

"That, my friend, is a very good question," Josie said, glancing over the edge of the boat to check for shoals. "You're clear on this side."

"Thanks," I said, slowly navigating closer. "The poor thing must be freaked out."

"She's not the only one," Josie said, making her way to the bow. "Just a couple feet closer."

I inched the boat forward, and Josie reached out with both hands. The beagle didn't put up much resistance and basically jumped into her arms. She sat down holding the dog, and I maneuvered the boat away from the buoy then turned the engine off. I joined them in the bow, and we did a cursory exam of the beagle.

"The poor thing is shaking. But she seems fine," Josie said, holding the beagle up with both hands to get a good look before setting her back down on her lap.

"How is this possible?" I said, frowning. "There's no way she could have climbed up there by herself."

"She's still damp," Josie said. "So, she's obviously been in the water. Do you think somebody was in the water with her and then lifted her onto the buoy?"

"Can you think of any other way she got up there?" I said.

"Maybe another boat dropped her off," Josie said, glancing around. "What does her name tag say?"

"There's no name tag," I said, removing the dog's collar. Then I studied the collar and noticed the writing embroidered into the leather. "Queen B."

The dog wagged her tail and cocked her head at the mention of her name.

"Queen B.?" Josie said, studying the dog. "Okay, now I get it. She's a Queen Elizabeth Pocket Beagle."

"That's the breed from medieval times that went extinct and has been recreated," I said, stroking the dog's ears. "They were taken on hunts and were so small they could fit in your coat pocket or saddlebag."

"That's the one," Josie said. "The first Queen Elizabeth apparently had a bunch of them. I think people started recreating the breed about fifteen years ago."

"She sure is cute," I said, scratching the dog's ears. "And tiny. What do you think she weighs?"

"Can't be more than ten pounds," Josie said, again scanning the water. "I don't see any other boats around."

"No, me either," I said. "Which means that someone was swimming and decided to put the dog on the buoy."

"Do you know how strange that sounds?" Josie said, frowning at me.

"It's definitely a ten on the weird scale," I said. "Can you come up with another explanation?"

"No, I can't," Josie said. "But if it was a swimmer, that means they were trying to save the dog's life."

"Because the swimmer was about to drown?"

"Yeah."

"I guess we should just take her home with us and wait to see if anything turns up," I said.

"Like a dead body?" Josie said, exhaling audibly.

"Oh, I sure hope not."

"Well, you have been looking for something to take your mind off the wedding."

"That would probably do it," I said as I sat down behind the wheel then started the engine and headed for home.

Chapter 2

I enjoyed the breeze and early morning sun as we made our way back to the Inn. Josie continued to comfort and pet the dog that was quickly recovering from its morning adventure. About a mile from Clay Bay, I noticed the local police boat anchored near Devil's Shoal, a notorious stretch of rock that ran several hundred yards and this spring was about a foot below the surface. Dozens of boaters, primarily tourists in rentals, ran aground on the shoal each summer usually losing the lower unit of their outboard motor in the process. But it was clear that Chief Abrams, Clay Bay's police chief, hadn't run aground. His boat was anchored next to the shoal, and he was talking with Freddie, our local medical examiner. I pulled up alongside the police boat and flinched when I saw the body bag on the deck.

"Good morning," Chief Abrams said.

"What happened?" I said, glancing down at the black body bag that was obviously occupied.

"I got a call about an hour ago," the Chief said. "Jerry Olsen was having breakfast on his deck when he saw a woman in the water who was struggling."

I glanced at Josie who stared back at me.

"Jerry said she was having a tough go of it and went down a couple of times before surfacing. Then she somehow managed to make it to the shoal. But just not in time."

"Who is she?" I said.

"No idea," the Chief said, shaking his head. "No identification and neither one of us recognize her. You guys want to take a look to see if you know her?"

"Not really," Josie said, shaking her head.

"If we must," I said with a grimace.

Freddie unzipped the bag about halfway, and we glanced down at a woman with bright red hair and a vacant stare who was probably somewhere in her forties. We both took a good look then shook our heads.

"No, I don't know her," I said. "Does she have any wounds or injuries?"

"It doesn't look like it," Freddie said. "Just a whole bunch of water in her lungs." Then he spotted the beagle. "Cute dog. A new addition to the family?"

"No, we just found her," I said.

"Out here?" the Chief said, frowning.

"She was perched on one of the channel markers," Josie said.

The Chief and Freddie looked at each other then focused on Josie.

"You were driving by and just happened to see her standing on a channel marker?" the Chief said.

"Yeah, that's pretty much it," Josie said. "Weird, huh?"

"How far upriver was it?" the Chief said.

"No more than a couple miles," Josie said. "I guess it could be the victim's dog, right?"

"She put her dog on a channel marker before she drowned?" the Chief said.

"The dog was wet," I said, still trying to make sense of what was going on. "Maybe she put the dog on the buoy and was planning to hold onto it until she got rescued."

"And then lost her grip and drifted off when the current grabbed her?" the Chief said, staring upriver. "I suppose it's possible."

"She must have fallen out of the boat she was in," Freddie said.

"Have you found a boat?" I said.

"No," the Chief said. "But I'm sure it'll turn up at some point."

"Unless it sunk," Freddie said with a shrug.

"You're on fire today, Freddie," Josie said.

"Yeah, thanks," Freddie said, frowning at her. "What are you going to do with the dog?"

"Just take her back to the Inn for now," I said. "Then we'll wait and see if anybody claims her."

"And if they do, you'll let me know straight away, right?" the Chief said.

"Of course," I said, then glanced at Josie. "You ready to get going?"

"Absolutely," she said. "Chef Claire said she was going to make French toast around ten."

"Don't rub it in," the Chief said. "We'll be lucky if we get a chance to eat lunch."

"Why don't you guys join us for dinner at C's?" I said. "My treat."

"And I suppose you'll be expecting an update?" the Chief said.

"You know me so well," I said, then pushed our boat away and started the engine.

We waved, then I checked my watch and accelerated.

Ten minutes later, the boat was docked, and we were heading up the path that led to the house. We entered the kitchen and found Chef Claire putting the finishing touches on a big stack of French toast sitting next to a plate of crisp bacon.

"Perfect timing," she said, then spotted the beagle. "Hey, she's a cutie. Where did you get her?"

Josie spent a few minutes telling her the story as we made short work of our breakfast. Then Chef Claire headed off to start her day at the restaurant, and Josie and I walked down the path to the Inn. We went in through the back door and saw Sammy hosing down the high-traffic tile walkway that ran in front of the dogs' condos. He turned the hose off when he saw the beagle and gently took her from Josie.

"Look at this girl," he beamed. "New family member or just a temporary guest?"

"TBD," Josie said. "I need to get ready for my eleven o'clock."

She headed for the registration area, and I glanced around at the empty condos.

"You plan on leaving the dogs outside most of the day?" I said.

"I thought I might," he said, handing me the beagle. "It's such a beautiful day."

"Yeah, good call," I said. "Are the house dogs outside with the rest of the gang?"

"They are," Sammy said. "Should I get a condo ready for the beagle?"

"Yeah, but let's leave her out for a while. She's had a tough morning. Why don't you come get her in my office around lunchtime?"

"Will do," he said, handing me the beagle before grabbing the hose.

I headed for my office and set the dog down on the couch. The beagle sat up on her haunches and cocked her head at me. I laughed when I saw the expectant look on her face and picked her up and set her down on my desk.

"You are an inquisitive little thing, aren't you?" I said, scratching her ears.

With the beagle watching my movements closely, I fired up my laptop then searched for the Pontilly Family Circus. I found their homepage and started scrolling. When I landed on the page that displayed photos of some of the featured acts, my initial suspicions were confirmed, and I immediately placed a call to Chief Abrams.

"Hey," he said. "How was breakfast?"

"Unbelievably good," I said. "She put chunks of fresh strawberries and pecans in the batter."

"Don't tell me that," he said.

"You asked."

"What's up?"

"Are you still out on the water?"

"No, we just docked, and they're removing the body as we speak."

"Why don't you swing by the Inn? I've got something to show you."

"I'm a little busy at the moment," he said. "Can it wait?"

"Sure," I said. "As long as you don't mind waiting to find out the identity of the dead woman."

"I'll be there in five."

I was still studying the circus's website when the Chief arrived. He sat down across from me and gently lifted the beagle onto his lap. He stroked her back until the dog rolled over. The Chief then began a tummy rub that soon lulled the dog to sleep.

"What do you have for me?"

"The dead woman is Samantha Pontilly," I said.

"Okay," the Chief said, frowning. "I assume you're going to tell me how you know that."

"Have a look," I said, turning the laptop toward him.

The Chief read from the screen then scrolled and read some more.

"A circus performer?"

"Her family's circus," I said. "That has just started a summer tour and is traveling by boat."

"Boat?" the Chief said.

"We saw the boat this morning," I said. "And then I saw someone throw something overboard. At the time, I assumed it was a garbage bag. But we were too far away to get a good look at what it was."

"And you think it was the woman and the beagle that were thrown off the boat," he said.

"It's the only thing that makes any sense," I said. "Right?"

"I guess," he said, frowning. "The website says she had a dog act."

"Yeah, Samantha's Pack of Wonder," I said. "It looks like there are nine dogs who perform all sorts of tricks. But I don't think the beagle is part of the act."

"I wonder why anybody would want to kill her," the Chief said.

"I have no idea," I said with a shrug. "But the Pontilly family has had their circus for close to a hundred years. They're now in their fourth generation. And Samantha was the daughter of the guy who runs it."

"And they're doing a summer tour up and down the River?" he said, shaking his head.

"They are," I said. "The family was originally based in Croatia, but most of the circuses with wild animal acts have been banned over there as well as a lot of other places they used to tour."

"So, they bought a boat and decided to tour the U.S. and Canada?"

"That's what it looks like. I can't believe they haven't been banned on both sides of the River by now," I said. "They still have elephant and big cat acts. Disgusting."

"Yeah, I've never been a fan of those," the Chief said. "I can only imagine what those animals must go through."

"The tour starts in Brockville in a few days," I said, grinning at him.

"You want to go to the circus?"

"Well, I would like to check it out just to see if anybody is looking for the dog."

"And do a little snooping while you're there?"

"Only if we have time," I said, giving him a coy smile.

"Promise me you won't do anything stupid if you see somebody mistreating one of those animals?" he said, raising an eyebrow at me.

"C'mon, Chief. You know I can't do that."

Chapter 3

At three o'clock, I met Josie in the registration area, and we headed outside to wait for the architect who was helping us design the rescue center we were building on the hundred acres of vacant land my mother owned directly behind the Inn. Apart from the fencing that was rapidly going up around the perimeter of the property and a large barn that was beginning to take shape, the spring rain and mud had slowed our progress, and we hadn't gotten as far along with our plans as we had hoped.

Truth be told, Josie and I hadn't made it any easier with our constant tweaks to the detailed drawings the architect had put together based on our earlier decisions. We were about to review round six that everyone hoped would be the final version.

We both waved when the architect, a local man named Stan Bule, parked in front of the Inn and hopped out carrying a set of rolled plans.

"Hey, Stan," I said, shaking hands with him. "Thanks for coming out again. Hopefully, this will the last time we put you through another round of changes."

"No problem," he said, grinning as he shook Josie's hand. "But I am happy I decided to bill this job by the hour."

We headed across the empty play area and opened the gate on the far side that led to the acreage. I closed the gate, and we waited for Stan to unroll the plans on a nearby tree stump.

"Okay, I think I've captured what you want," he said. "And I like your idea of putting walking paths throughout the place. Visitors will be able to get up close and personal. Assuming that you won't have dangerous critters wandering loose around the property."

"No, we won't," I said, glancing at Josie. "That's what the caged areas are for."

"So, if I bring my kids out for the day, I won't have to worry about them coming face to face with a black bear?"

"Only through a thick set of bars," Josie said. "Were you able to make the changes we wanted to those?"

"I was," he said, pointing at the plans. "I increased the size of the large animal areas to an acre each, but I had to cut the number down to a dozen. But I was able to keep the acre you wanted for raccoons and other critters."

"Good," I said. "We expect to get a lot of stray or injured small animals."

"That's going to be one big cage," he said.

"Well, you know how Josie is," I said. "She needs her space."

"Funny," Josie said.

"And to get the overall look and feel you want, you're going to have to build several barriers and some additional security fencing. It's not going to be cheap."

"Yeah, we know," I said. "Fortunately, my mother is on a bit of a spending spree at the moment."

"I heard," he said, laughing. "An eight-foot ice sculpture of the happy couple?"

"How did you hear about it?" I said, frowning.

"I got it from Freddie, who got it from Chief Abrams, who got it from your mom," Stan said.

"News travels fast," Josie said.

"C'mon, let's walk over to the pond," Stan said, rolling up the plans. "I think you're going to like what I did with it."

We followed him and walked until I was breathing heavily and dripping sweat even though the temperature was in the mid-sixties. Eventually, we came to a stop at the edge of an enormous, spring-fed pond that sat in the middle of the property. When Josie and I had first begun talking about the rescue center, we hadn't put much thought into how the pond might be incorporated into the overall plan. But at Chef Claire's suggestion, since fish and birds were such a big part of our local wildlife, we decided the center should highlight them. Stan again unrolled the plans, and we sat down at the edge of the pond to review his latest version.

"If I were you, I'd stock the pond and let the kids fish," he said. "And it won't take much to attract all sorts of waterfowl.

Add in a bunch of squirrels and some tame deer, and you've got yourself something special."

"What are those things?" Josie said, pointing at several notations on the plan that appeared to be sitting in the middle of the pond.

"Those are the aerators we talked about," he said. "They'll help maintain the oxygen levels and keep the pond ice-free in the winter."

"Cool," I said, nodding as I studied the plan. "And what's that thing on the other side of the pond?"

"You mentioned that it might be nice if people had a chance to kick back and maybe have a picnic while they're here. So, I thought we might build a natural amphitheater on the bank on the far side," Stan said. "You do realize that it's turning into a nature reserve as much as a rescue center, right?"

"We thought we'd try to do both," I said. "And we should be fine as long as we only put animals out here that won't eat each other."

"Or people," Josie deadpanned.

"Yeah, thanks for the safety tip," I said, making a face at her. "I like it, Stan."

"Yeah, me too," Josie said. "So, what's the next step?"

"Finish all the fencing, get a couple of dozers in here to move some dirt around, and then turn all your summer hires loose with rakes and shovels," he said, rolling up the plan. "And you'll need an experienced crew to handle the construction of the cages. A black bear or a mountain lion getting loose and prowling around out here is not a good idea."

We walked back to the Inn, said our goodbyes to Stan then headed inside where Chloe and Captain were rolling around on the floor with Queen B. The Newfie playfully draped one of his enormous paws over the beagle, and she almost disappeared from sight. I glanced at Jill who was watching the dogs from behind the registration counter.

"How are they getting along?" I said.

"They're doing great," Jill said. "What are you going to do with the beagle? Sammy and I have been talking about getting another dog, and she is adorable."

"We'll let you know as soon as we can," I said. "Hopefully, as soon as we get back from the circus."

"Okay," Jill said, staring at me like I'd lost my mind. She turned to Josie. "Should I even ask?"

"Probably not," Josie said, shaking her head. "Are you guys all set here? The Ringmaster and I need to get ready for dinner."

"Yeah, we're good," Jill said. "But your schedule is packed tomorrow. You start with an eight o'clock spaying."

"I'll be here," Josie said, heading for the back door. "Enjoy your evening."

"Would it be okay if we took the beagle home with us tonight?"

Josie and I looked at each other and shrugged.

"Sure, why not?" she said. "Have fun."

We headed up to the house to shower and change then drove to C's. I parked in back, and we entered through the kitchen where Chef Claire was in the middle of a conversation about the evening's specials with her staff. She gave us a brief wave then we headed for the lounge and took a seat at the bar. Millie, our head bartender, greeted us with a big smile then poured two glasses of wine. I took a sip and glanced around. Then I noticed the look on Josie's face and followed her eyes to the front door where my mother was chatting with our hostess.

"Get ready," Josie said.

"Yeah, I'll do my best," I said, staring at the object she was holding under one of her arms.

"Is that what I think it is?" Josie said.

"Yeah, she brought the binder with her," I said, shaking my head.

"The dreaded binder," Josie whispered. "Ten bucks she wants to talk about flowers tonight."

"You're on," I said. "Since we're in the restaurant, her mind is going to be on food. She's gonna want to talk appetizers."

Chapter 4

I glanced up from my menu and noticed that my mother had both hands on top of the binder as if she were protecting a puppy from falling off her lap. I did my best to ignore the expectant look she was giving me and refocused on my dinner choices. Freddie and Chief Abrams strolled across the dining room and sat down.

"What's everyone having?" Chief Abrams said.

"I think I'm going to go Italian tonight," I said, sliding my menu aside.

My mother voiced her displeasure with a quick intake of air.

"Yes?" I said, staring at her.

"Nothing," my mother said.

I waited out the ensuing silence.

"It's just that I'm not sure that someone who wants to fit into her wedding dress should be eating all those carbs."

"I'm stress eating," I said.

"What on earth do you have to be stressed about?" she said, drumming her fingers on top of the binder.

Everyone at the table glanced over at my mother then at each other with a grin. I let her question pass without comment, and our server approached to take our orders. When he departed, my mother flipped the binder open and leaned forward.

"Before our food gets here, I thought we'd take a few minutes to discuss a couple of items," she said.

"What's it going to be tonight, Mom?"

"Let's start with appetizers," she said, handing me a piece of paper.

I smiled at Josie and held my hand out. She shook her head and placed a ten-dollar bill in my palm.

"Sweet," I said, tossing the ten on the table. "Thanks for playing."

"What did I miss?" my mother said, frowning.

"We had a bet on what you wanted to talk about," Josie said. "I went with flowers."

"They're next on the list," my mother said, tapping the binder.

"Ha," Josie said, snatching the ten back and sliding it into her pocket.

My stomach rumbled as I scanned the impressive collection of appetizers then slid the page across the table.

"That looks like a great list, Mom," I said. "I assume you worked on it with Chef Claire."

"Of course. They're all one-bite items," she said. "I wanted to avoid having to use cutlery before dinner."

"Good call. You probably don't want me holding a knife that day," I said, then focused on Freddie. "Any update on the Pontilly woman?"

"Nothing new," Freddie said.

"Pontilly?" my mother said. "Like the circus?"

"Yeah," I said, frowning at her. "How did you know that?"

"They called the town council offices a few days ago," she said. "Apparently, one of their tour stops canceled, and they're looking to fill the slot."

"What did you tell them?" I said.

"I didn't tell them anything," my mother said. "I was busy shopping for wedding invitations. Remind me to show you some samples after dinner."

"Sure, sure," I said, nodding. "Is the Council thinking about booking them?"

"I'm not sure," she said, then raised an eyebrow at me. "Why do you care? You hate circuses."

"No, I don't," I said. "I just don't like circuses that have wild animal acts. You should book them."

"Let's back up a second," my mother said, glancing around the table. "What sort of update are you talking about?"

"You heard about the drowning this morning, right?" the Chief said.

"I did. Simply tragic. And a horrible way to start the season."

"The victim was a woman by the name of Samantha Pontilly," the Chief said. "She was the daughter of the guy who runs the circus."

"And the family contacted you?" my mother said, taking a sip of wine.

"No, in fact, we haven't heard a word from them," he said. "I've been trying to get in touch with them all day, but the main number that's listed on their website appears to be disconnected. And I have to say that made me a bit suspicious. I eventually called the Brockville police this afternoon. They said they'd head over to the circus and deliver the news that we found her body."

"How did you know who the poor woman was?" my mother said.

"Suzy figured it out," the Chief said.

"Of course, she did," my mother said, shaking her head. "Unbelievable."

"It was easy. We found her dog on a channel buoy and put two and two together," I said.

"Her dog was on a channel marker?" my mother said, bewildered.

"Yeah," I said. "We saw their boat earlier, then found the dog. And we ran into the Chief and Freddie on our way home when they were recovering the body. Samantha's photos were all over their website." I turned to Chief Abrams. "So, nobody contacted you about a missing person?"

"Nope," he said with a shrug.

"Weird," I said, then focused on my mother. "When's the open date on their schedule?"

"I believe it's around the middle of June," she said. "You can't be serious about us booking a circus."

"Why not?" I said. "The kids will love it."

Josie snorted.

"Shut it."

"Even though they have animal acts?" my mother said.

"I'll just step outside while they're going on," I said, my mind racing. "And since we have her dog, we need to see if there's someone there who wants to take her."

"We don't need to bring the circus to town to do that, darling. A simple phone call will do the trick."

"C'mon, Mom," I said, patting her hand. "It'll be fun."

"Yeah, and we wouldn't want to disappoint the kids," Josie deadpanned.

"You're not helping," I said, glaring at her.

"Disagree."

"Well, we have been looking for a way to add an event between Memorial Day and the Fourth of July," my mother said. "But we really don't have much time. There's so much to do."

"You and the rest of the council can handle it, Mom," I said. "You guys have done things on short notice before."

My mother fell silent and stared off into the distance for several moments. Then she focused on me.

"Promise me you'll be on your best behavior?"

"Of course," I said. "I'm surprised you even have to ask."

Everyone at the table burst into laughter. I sat back in my chair as I waited it out.

"So, what do you say?"

"I guess it could work," she said, then her face morphed into an evil grin. "Besides, stealing an elephant would be much harder than kidnapping some roosters."

Her comment was the latest addition to her repartee related to my recent arrest in Cayman where Josie and I, along with our good friend, Rooster, had kidnapped a bunch of roosters from an illegal cockfight. Even though the local police had dropped all the charges along with the threat of deportation, my mother continued to harangue me on a regular basis about what she called my most recent *descent into madness*.

"You're never gonna let that one go, are you?" I said.

"Not until you give me something better to work with," she said, laughing.

"Like kidnapping an elephant," Josie said.

"That would do it," my mother said, nodding.

"Okay, Mom. I promise not to kidnap the elephant. So, what do you say?"

"I guess it could be fun. Let me go make a couple of calls," she said, grabbing her phone and getting up from the table.

"Well played," Josie said after my mother had disappeared into the lounge.

"What?"

"It's a two for one," Josie said, dipping a piece of Italian bread into a saucer of olive oil. "The circus comes to town giving you a chance to do some serious snooping, and it takes her mind off the wedding preparations for a few weeks."

"Oh, you caught that," I said, grinning at her.

"Yeah, it wasn't that tough," she said, reaching for another piece of bread. "I didn't even need my glove."

Chapter 5

After learning that the circus's performance in Brockville was an afternoon matinee, we decided to make the trip by boat. Brockville's a Canadian town of around 25,000 that sits on the eastern edge of the Thousand Islands and is less than a leisurely one-hour ride from Clay Bay. The weather was perfect, and Josie and I were lounging in the bow of Rooster's boat snacking from a picnic basket sitting between us on the seat. Rooster and Chief Abrams were chatting near the stern with Rooster behind the wheel.

"Great idea to come by boat," Josie said, sliding her ponytail through the opening in the back of the Blue Jays hat she was wearing.

"It's a gorgeous day," I said, reaching for another bacon wrapped chicken tender. "I thought we'd introduce ourselves to the family and see if we can sneak a peek at how they're treating the animals."

"Or we could just enjoy the show," she said, lowering her sunglasses to make eye contact.

"Oh, I'm sure we'll see the show," I said, then shrugged. "Or at least most of it."

"If you plan on doing something crazy, how about you just wait until they come to town?" Josie said.

"Yeah, good idea. Homefield advantage," I said, nodding.

Josie shook her head then dug through the picnic basket.

We parked the boat at the town docks then made the short walk. An enormous circus tent was set up not far from downtown, and a good-sized crowd was already filing in. I handed my ticket to the attendant then stepped inside the tent and looked around.

"I'm going to see if I can find Mr. Pontilly," I said, continuing to scan the tent.

"Why?" Chief Abrams said, frowning at me.

I reached into my bag and pulled out a document and waved it in the air.

"Because he needs to sign the contract," I said, grinning.

"Unbelievable," Josie said, shaking her head. "Your mother asked you to get the contract signed?"

"No," I said, glancing away. "I thought I'd surprise her."

"Why am I starting to get a bad feeling about this?" Josie said, glancing back and forth at Rooster and the Chief.

"I would have thought you'd be used to it by now," the Chief said, then fixed his stare on me. "Try to take it easy on him. He just lost his daughter."

"Of course," I said. "I'm not a total idiot. Where are you guys going to be sitting?"

"As far away from the clowns as possible," Josie said.

"That's right, I forgot," I said, laughing. "You're scared of clowns."

"I'm not scared. They just sort of freak me out," she said, then sniffed the air. "Ooh, I smell funnel cakes."

"Me too," I said, taking a look around. "Grab me one while you're at it. I'll be right back."

I waved over my shoulder as I headed for the other side of the tent. A man wearing a ridiculous lime green tuxedo was standing in front of a section of the tent cordoned off by a set of curtains. He gave me a blank stare as I approached.

"Hi," I said. "Nice tux. Love the color."

"You're joking, right?" he said with a scowl.

"Yeah, I am," I said with a chuckle. "They actually make you wear that thing?"

"Welcome to the circus," he said without emotion. "Do you want something?"

"I need to see Mr. Pontilly."

"He's getting ready for the show," he said, not budging.

"I have a contract he needs to sign," I said, holding out the document. "It's for your upcoming performance in Clay Bay."

"I'll have him sign it and get it back to you before you leave," he said, reaching for the contact.

"No, that's okay," I said, snatching it back. "There are a few things I need to go over with him."

He stared at me then nodded.

"Okay, but be quick," he said, pulling the curtains far enough apart for me to squeeze through. "He's in the wardrobe room. Halfway down on the left."

"Thanks," I said, working my way through the opening.

I glanced around and noticed several performers in costume milling around. A man and a woman wearing skintight leotards were doing elaborate stretching exercises that hurt just to watch. Several more were on unicycles and juggling. Off to one side, a man wearing a white suit accented with embroidered gold lame was repeatedly cracking a long whip. I recognized him from his picture on the website and hated him at first sight.

Master Claude, head animal trainer and exalted tamer of wild beasts on four continents.

What a load of crap.

Before I had time to dream up all the different items I might be able to use on Master Claude as payback, I saw two clowns walking toward me in full costume. They were both smoking and took final drags before tossing their cigarettes on the dirt floor and crushing them out with their enormous clown feet.

"Hey," I said to both of them as they got close. "Are you guys heading out to entertain the crowd?"

"No," one of the clowns deadpanned through what could have been a frown. "We're actually on our way to the hospital. We're cardiologists."

"Everybody's a comedian," I said, frowning at them. "How would you like to make fifty bucks each?"

"Keep talking," the other clown said. He was wearing a multi-colored wig, and his painted face reminded me of a deranged villain you might see in a horror movie. "I'm sure the guy's heart will keep beating for a while, right, Bubs?"

The clown named Bubs laughed.

"Good one, Chuckles," he said, then focused on me. "What do we need to do for the fifty bucks?"

"I want you to hover around my friend," I said, glancing back and forth at them.

"Hover?" Bubs said. "In these shoes?"

They both laughed again, and I waited it out.

"She's got a thing about clowns," I said. "If you know what I mean."

"Yeah, we get them all the time," Chuckles said. "People like that give clowns a bad name."

"Sure, sure," I said, nodding. "All you have to do is walk up behind her. Or if you get a chance, sit down on either side of her. But don't say anything. Just give her your best clown look."

"Okay," Bubs said. "But there's probably a thousand people here. How are we going to find her?"

"It shouldn't be hard," I said. "She's wearing dark blue shorts and a yellow blouse. And she's wearing a Blue Jays baseball cap with her ponytail hanging out the back. Right now, you'll find her in line for funnel cakes."

The two clowns looked at each other and nodded. I handed them a hundred-dollar bill.

"Thanks," I said with an evil grin. "This is gonna be a hoot." Then I frowned when they didn't move. "Shouldn't you get going?"

"You're standing on my foot," Bubs said.

"Oh, sorry about that," I said, lifting my foot off his gigantic black shoe. "Remember, don't say a word."

"Got it," Chuckles said.

"And there's an extra hundred in it if you get a scream out of her."

I pulled one of the side curtains back and poked my head through the opening. I watched both clowns head off then glanced around. I spied the funnel cake stand and saw Josie near the end of the line staring down at her phone. Bubs and Chuckles slipped into line directly behind her, and it looked like one of the clowns nudged her ankle with his shoe. Josie slowly turned around then dropped her phone and screamed. She bent down to snatch the phone off the ground, briefly stared at the clowns with her face contorted in panic, then made a beeline for Rooster and the Chief who were sitting in the stands nearby.

I chortled and handed a hundred to the guy in the lime green tux.

"Could you make sure that gets to Bubs and Chuckles?"

"For ten bucks, sure," he said, staring at the bill.

"Ten bucks just to hand it over?"

"Hey, times are tough," he said with a shrug.

I dug a ten out of my pocket and handed it to him then made my way to the wardrobe room. I stepped inside and saw a tiny man with white hair wearing a red, white and blue costume highlighted with an elaborate set of tails. He was staring into a mirror directly in front of him and applying makeup. I put him somewhere deep into his eighties, perhaps even older.

Then I remembered the loss of his daughter and felt a wave of sympathy wash over me.

"Mr. Pontilly?"

He glanced at me in the mirror then turned around.

"The one and only," he said with a thick accent as he got to his feet. The top of his head barely reached my shoulders, and for the first time in ages, I almost felt tall. "How can I help you?"

"It's nice to meet you," I said. "I'm Suzy Chandler."

"Chandler?" he said with a frown. "Why does that name ring a bell?"

"You've been talking to my mother about your upcoming performance in Clay Bay."

"Of course, that's it," he said, giving me the once-over. "She said she was going to be emailing the contract."

"I have it with me," I said, digging the document out of my bag and handing it to him.

"You didn't need to come all the way here," he said, flipping through the pages.

"We wanted to see the show," I said, then remembered. "I'm so sorry about your daughter."

"Thank you," he said. "A tragic accident. But Sammy wasn't my daughter."

"She wasn't?" I said. "But that's what it says on your website."

"Do you make it a habit of believing everything you read online, Ms. Chandler?"

"No," I said, shaking my head. "Actually, I have a tendency to disbelieve until I'm convinced otherwise."

"That's a good approach," he said. "Our name is the Pontilly *Family* Circus. And if I take some liberties with the definition of family, I'm quite sure people will forgive me."

"So, how many family members actually work in the circus?" I said, folding my arms as I leaned against a metal post.

"None," he said with a sad smile. "I'm the only one left. I'm afraid the Pontilly lineage has just about run its course. And it ends when I go."

"That's so sad. I'm sorry to hear that."

"What's that old saying?" he said. "It is what it is."

"Was Samantha her real name?"

"It was," he said. "But her last name was Johnson."

"Was she also from Croatia?"

"Oh, no," he said, shaking his head. "Sammy was an all-American girl." Then he chuckled softly. "She had such a hard time getting the accent right. Actually, the summer River tour was her idea. She grew up not far from here."

"Really? Do you know where?"

"I do not," he said. "Sammy didn't like to talk much about her past. But I always assumed her childhood was difficult given her decision."

"What decision was that?" I said, frowning.

"Why her decision to run away and join the circus, what else?"

"Yeah. Got it," I said with a smile and a shrug. "Duh."

The old man laughed and focused on the contract. I waited patiently for him to review it, then he grabbed a pen from the table.

"This looks fine," he said, then signed and dated the last page. "You'll make sure this gets back to your mother?"

"I will," I said, trying to decide how many more questions I had time for before the show began. "What's going to happen to the circus after...you're no longer capable of running it?"

"You mean after I kick the bucket?" he said, grinning.

"Yeah."

"There's an old saying in my country," he said. "The dead have no need to fear or worry about the future." Then he shrugged. "It sounds better in Croatian."

"I don't speak Croatian," I said, shaking my head.

"That's why I said it in English," he said with a big smile.

"At the risk of repeating myself," I said, my face flushing with embarrassment. "Duh."

"Indeed," he said with a big grin. "Now, if you'll excuse me, I have a show to do."

38

"Can I ask you one more question?"

"Go right ahead," he said, putting on a top hat and tightening the strap under his chin.

"Don't you think it's barbaric to use wild animals in some of your acts?"

"Barbaric? Strong word," he said, his eyes narrowing. "I assure you that our animals are well taken care of."

"I'm not so sure the animals would agree with you," I said, returning his stare.

"Wild animals require exhaustive training and close supervision, Ms. Chandler."

"Only when they're in captivity."

"Yes," he said, nodding. "Only when in captivity."

"Why do you keep using them?"

"Circus tradition, primarily," he said, shrugging. "I really need to go. Can't keep the public waiting, right?"

"Yeah," I said, then brightened. "And we'll be seeing you soon in Clay Bay."

"You will indeed," he said, taking a final look at himself in the mirror. "Oh, since we're so close to showtime, you should probably go out through the back. You'll be able to make your way to your seat from there. Just turn left and follow the path."

"Okay," I said, extending my hand. "It was nice meeting you, Mr. Pontilly. And I'm very sorry about what happened to Samantha."

"Thank you," he said, then took a couple of quick, deep breaths and headed for the curtains with an energetic stride.

"Not bad for an old man," I said, admiring his vitality.

Then I looked at the group of performers assembled near the curtain, wheeled around and exited through the back. I glanced up and down the dirt path. I was just about to take a step in the direction that would lead me back to my seat but stopped.

Then I made a right.

I casually strolled past a couple of workers who were sitting near two large cages that each contained an enormous tiger. I bit my lip and kept walking. But when I saw the man in the white suit with his back to me, my base instincts took control. He had swapped out the whip for a bullhook and was using it to get an elephant to do his bidding by putting the hooked end of the long pole behind the elephant's ear. It was obvious he was hurting the elephant, and I noticed spattered blood on the ground.

Enraged, I was about to punch the guy in the head when I noticed a cattle prod sitting on a stool. The instrument was basically a taser on a long pole, and I decided it would be much better used on the guy in the suit than it would the elephant. I crept up to the stool and grabbed the cattle prod then continued my stealthy approach. He still had his back to me and was obviously annoyed with the recalcitrant beast. But the elephant saw me and made and maintained eye contact. I took another step closer then jabbed the man's back with the cattle prod. I'm not sure how many volts surged through his body, but he dropped the bullhook, spasmed, then dropped to his knees before falling face first into the dirt.

I tossed the cattle prod on the ground next to the twitching man then slowly extended my hand and stroked the elephant's trunk.

"I wish I could do more," I said to the gentle giant.

I quickly got the heck out of Dodge and headed around the back of the grandstand and finally spotted my three companions sitting at the end of a row. Josie patted the spot she had saved, and I sat down between her and Rooster.

"Where have you been?" Josie said.

"Oh, just clowning around," I said, grinning at her.

She looked at me, then her eyes narrowed.

"I knew it was you," she said. "Those two scared the crap out of me."

"So, I noticed," I said, laughing. "Where's my funnel cake?"

"Bite me," she said. "What's it like back there?"

"About what you'd expect. Smelly and dirty with lots of people doing things with their bodies I didn't believe were possible," I said, reaching for a handful of peanuts from the bag she was holding. "The old man who runs it is interesting."

I glanced out at the aerialists who were swinging high in the air above a large net and doing somersaults.

"That's pretty cool," I said. "They're good."

"Yeah, they are," Josie said, cracking a shell and tossing the peanut into her mouth. "Apparently, they'll be back again after intermission. But I'm not looking forward to the animal acts."

"I doubt if they're going to be doing the animal acts today," I said, continuing to watch the action high above the ground.

"Why's that?" she said, glancing over at me.

"Because I just shot the trainer," I whispered.

"You shot him?"

"Well, shot may be a bit of an overstatement. But I did get him right in the back."

"With what?

"An electric cattle prod."

"Did it knock him out?"

"Oh, yeah. It certainly did. When I left, he was taking a dirt nap."

"Did anybody see you?" Josie said.

"No, I don't think so," I said.

"Well done. Good for you."

"Yeah, thanks. I thought you'd appreciate it."

Chapter 6

Four days had passed since I'd rendered Master Claude to a voltage-induced, spasming collection of flesh and dirt, and since no cops from either side of the border had shown up to arrest me, it appeared that my expertise with a cattle prod would remain a secret. Neither one of us had felt the need to share my exploits with Chief Abrams or Rooster, but they both kept giving me strange looks on the ride home when they noticed the contented grin I couldn't get rid of.

Since then, I'd become interested or, as Josie called it, obsessed with tracking down information that might lead me to family members or acquaintances of the late Samantha Johnson. I didn't have much to go on other than Mr. Pontilly's remark about her growing up somewhere around the Islands. There were hundreds of small towns and hamlets dotting upstate New York, but at least I was able to eliminate Canadian towns from my search based on Pontilly's comment about Samantha being an all-American girl. But my search continued to be a frustrating, fruitless effort that only intensified my desire to figure out who the heck she was and where she came from.

Not to mention getting a handle on why somebody had thrown her and the dog off the boat.

I closed my laptop and grabbed a bag of bite-sized from a drawer and put my feet up on the desk. I glanced out the window at the play area where the dogs were enjoying the warm weather. I popped one of the bite-sized and looked at the stack of paperwork I needed to take care of before I knocked off for the day. The busy season had arrived at the Inn, and we were almost at capacity. But I was having a hard time concentrating on work given my interest in the dead woman that was Samantha Johnson-Pontilly.

Okay, I'll fess up.

I was officially obsessed.

Josie entered the office wearing her scrubs and plopped down on the couch and stretched out. I held up the bag of bite-sized.

"Maybe just a couple," she said, then caught the bag. "You're not supposed to be eating these things before the wedding."

"Did my mother tell you to remind me?"

"She did," Josie said, laughing as she unwrapped one of the morsels. "My work is done."

I shook my head at my mother's relentless efforts and removed my feet from the desk. I caught the bag when Josie threw it back and tossed it into the drawer.

"I sure hope nobody from the circus wants Queen B. back," Josie said. "It would break Sammy and Jill's heart."

"Yeah, they've really bonded," I said. "I should have asked around when we were at the circus. But I completely forgot."

"You were a little busy that night," Josie said. "Dealing with the contract, assaulting Master Claude…bribing clowns to do your bidding."

"Just let it go," I said, laughing. "It was a harmless prank."

"I'm still having nightmares," she said. "But don't worry, your day is coming."

"Thanks for the warning."

"Oh, it's a promise," she said, popping a bite-sized.

The office door opened, and Chief Abrams strolled in.

"Hey, Chief," I said.

"Hi, guys," he said, then motioned for Josie not to get up. He sat down in a chair on the other side of the desk. "I figured you guys would be out on the River today. It's beautiful out."

"I just came out of my third surgery of the day," Josie said. "And I still have one to go."

"And I've got a ton of paperwork to deal with that I've been putting off," I said. "Have you had any luck?"

"Not a bit," he said, shaking his head. "I checked the State's birth records back to 1970 and found forty-nine Samantha Johnsons."

"That's a start," I said, leaning forward.

"Nah, it's a total washout," he said, shaking his head. "Two dozen of them are under twenty-one, five are deceased, nineteen are married, and the other one is currently serving a twenty-year sentence."

"How hard would it be to check other states?" I said.

"Do you have any idea how many Johnson families there are around the country?" the Chief said, raising an eyebrow at me.

"I could probably ballpark it," I said with a shrug.

Josie snorted. I ignored her and looked across the desk at Chief Abrams.

"She must have been born in another state, and her parents moved to the area when she was young," I said.

"Or Pontilly got it wrong," the Chief said.

"I don't think so," I said. "He's still sharp as a tack."

"Maybe the woman lied about where she was from," Josie said, sitting up on the couch and folding her legs underneath her.

"But why would she do that?" I said.

"Who knows?" Josie said with a shrug. "But she did run away to join the circus. It's not what I'd call normal behavior. Maybe she had a good reason for creating a cover story about her background."

"That makes the most sense," the Chief said.

"Did you check with the DMV?" I said.

"I did. No driver's license or car registration."

"Did you also check the name Samantha Pontilly?"

"Yes," he said, nodding. "And if she did legally change her name, she didn't do it in this state."

"Missing person database?"

"Nothing there."

"Criminal records?"

"Just the one doing twenty for manslaughter."

"Phone records?"

"She had a cell phone the circus provided," the Chief said.

"Any interesting numbers come up in the call history?" I said.

The Chief exhaled and glanced at Josie.

"Is it just me, or does she exhaust you as well?"

"Rhetorical, right?"

"Funny," I said, giving both of them a dirty look.

"Apparently, Samantha wasn't much of a talker," he said. "At least on the phone. There were just a handful of calls. And nothing in the 315 area code. Or any other New York area codes for that matter."

"This is really starting to annoy me," I said.

"Now you know how we feel," Josie said, grinning at me.

I ignored her and started drumming my fingers on the desk.

"What's left?" I said.

"Church records?" Josie said.

"There are hundreds, maybe thousands of churches around the region," Chief Abrams said. "And there's obviously no centralized database of church membership."

"Schools?" I said.

"Sure, if she went to a school in the area, it would be there," he said. "But it's the same problem we have with the churches. Without the name of the town, there's no way to track her down."

I sat back in my chair as an idea floated to the surface.

"Library archives," I said, nodding.

"Same problem as the schools and churches," the Chief said.

"Yes," I said, grinning. "Except we have a secret weapon in our library."

"Are you talking about Ms. McTavish?" Chief Abrams said.

"I am."

"Oh, she doesn't like me," Josie said.

"That's because she caught you sneaking food into the reading room," I said.

"She was really mean," Josie said. "And she's a confiscator."

"Don't worry about it," I said. "She's caught me at least a dozen times with food. Fortunately, she doesn't hold a grudge."

"How do you think she can help?" the Chief said.

"I remember her telling me about her effort to maintain a comprehensive history of the region," I said. "And I think she started subscribing to every newspaper within a couple hundred miles and then microfilming them."

"I assume we're talking about a time before the internet?" the Chief said.

"Oh, way before," I said. "And I think she also microfilmed every school yearbook she could find."

"That sounds like an awful lot of work, Suzy," the Chief said. "I doubt if an old system like that even has a keyword search. We'd probably have to go through each item."

"That could take days," Josie said.

"You got a better idea?" I said, glancing back and forth at them.

"Every idea I have is better than that," Josie said.

"C'mon, it'll be fun," I said. "Just think of all the local history we're going to learn."

Josie and Chief Abrams looked at each other with blank stares.

"Do you think it's worth putting up a fight before she eventually wears us down?" the Chief said.

"Based on past history," Josie said. "I'm gonna go with no."

"Yeah, that's what I thought. Okay, Snoopmeister, I'm in," the Chief said. "But if we hit a dead end, you have to promise that you'll let it go."

"Sure, sure," I said, nodding. "But I've got a good feeling about this one."

Chapter 7

We climbed the short set of steps in front of the ivy-covered library, and I held the door open for Josie and the Chief. The librarian, a tiny, white-haired woman who was eighty-five if she was a day, peered over the top of the counter and squinted at us through thick glasses then beamed when she recognized us. To local residents, Ms. McTavish was almost as much of an attraction as the River, and we all loved her to death. At least twenty years past the time when she could have retired, she continued to work five days a week, her workload lightened by two part-time workers the town council had provided several years ago.

When I was still in my teens, I had once asked my mother why Ms. McTavish hadn't retired. My mother had responded in no uncertain terms that the librarian, who'd remained single her entire life, lived for the job. And since taking it away could also mean the end of Ms. McTavish, there was no way she or the rest of the town council were going to take that chance.

We headed for the front counter, and she came out from behind the desk to greet us. She tilted her head back and looked up at us with a big smile.

"Hi, Ms. McTavish," I said, giving her a gentle hug.

"Suzy, it's so good to see you," she said. "I haven't seen you in a while, and I was worried you might be getting behind in your reading."

"No, I try to read a chapter a night, just like you taught me," I said.

"A chapter a day keeps the cobwebs away," she said, holding up a finger to emphasize her point. "Hi, Josie. Chief Abrams."

"How are you doing?" the Chief said, placing both hands over one of hers.

"Oh, I'm fine," she said with a well-practiced wink. "I think I've lost a step, but don't worry, I'm sure it'll turn up somewhere."

We all laughed at the familiar joke.

"Hi, Ms. McTavish," Josie said, also giving her a hug. "You look great."

"Hello, dear," she said, affectionately squeezing Josie's hand. "I was getting ready to close for the evening, but I'd be happy to help you find something."

"Actually, Ms. McTavish," I said. "We're not here to borrow any books. We're looking for some information."

"Okay. How can I help you?"

I spent a few minutes summarizing the situation, and she listened closely.

"I heard about the drowning. What a horrible way for a life to end. And you say that you have no idea who she was?"

"Well, we know what's she been doing for the past several years, but we have no idea where she grew up apart from the fact that it was probably somewhere close to the River," the Chief said.

"What has she been doing?" the librarian said.

"She was a circus performer," the Chief said. "She had a dog act."

"I see," Ms. McTavish said, nodding. "And the circus doesn't know the background of one of their own long-term employees?"

"Apparently, she didn't like to talk about it," I said.

"I see. This circus wouldn't happen to be the same one that's coming to town," she said, giving me a coy smile."

"How the heck did you know that?" I said.

"Dear, I may have lost a step, but I'm not a doddering idiot," she said, chuckling. "And your reputation proceeds you." She glanced around at all three of us. "You suspect foul play, don't you?"

"We do," the Chief said after an extended pause. "And we'd like to find out if she has any family members in the area. They need to know what's happened to her."

"Of course," the librarian said. "What time period are we looking at?"

"Our best guess is somewhere between 1970 and the mid-80s," the Chief said.

"Before the internet," she said, shaking her head. "That's going to make it much harder."

"Do you still have your microfilm library?" I said.

"I do," she said. "But I'm afraid you would have to review each item individually. The search capabilities of that system are very limited."

"That's what we were afraid of," the Chief said. "But you wouldn't mind if we took a look, right?"

"Of course not," she said. "That's why I put it together. No one has used it for quite a while. In fact, I put it in the basement several years ago to make room for the computers."

"Do you have some sort of directory?" I said. "You know, a list of the school districts and the towns they include. And maybe the same sort of thing for all the newspapers."

"I do," she said, nodding. "It was the only way I could figure out how to organize all the information. When would you like to get started?"

"Tonight," the Chief said.

"Tonight?" she said, surprised.

"If you don't mind," he said. "Given our schedules, evenings are the only time we have available."

She stared at the Chief as she pondered the idea of having three people walking around her library unsupervised.

"Well, if I can't trust the chief of police, I'm in a whole lot of trouble, right?" she said, laughing. "Okay, I'll leave you a key in case you need it. Just remember to make sure it's locked up tight, and the alarm is set before you leave." Then she shrugged. "Unless you're still here when I come back in the morning. It's a whole lot of information."

She gestured for us to follow her behind the front counter and toward a set of stairs that led down to the basement. Then she stopped and turned around to glance back and forth at Josie and me.

"Oh, but first, hand them over," she said, gesturing with both hands.

"What?" I said, going for confused.

"You know what I'm talking about," she said, not budging.

I glanced at Josie, then we both nodded at Ms. McTavish and reached into our coats. I handed over three enormous sandwiches. Josie gave her a bag of chips and a Ziploc bag stuffed with cheese and olives. We glanced down at the floor when she gave us her best disapproving stare.

"What am I going to do with you two?" she said, shaking her head.

"Sorry."

"Yeah, sorry, Ms. McTavish," I said, then took a step toward the stairs. "We'll get started now."

"Hang on," she said, still planted directly in front of the top step. She repeated the hand gesture. "Don't forget the bite-sized."

"Ah, geez, Ms. McTavish," Josie said, reaching behind her back. She pulled out a fresh bag of bite-sized Snickers and handed it over.

The librarian turned her attention to me. I lost the staredown and removed a bag from my coat and gave it to her.

"Thank you," the librarian said, then focused on the Chief.

"I'm clean," the Chief said, showing her both hands.

"Okay," she said. "If I'm not feeling peckish later tonight, you can pick them up in the morning. Just head down to the basement, and you'll find the directory next to the display terminals. I'll lock up behind me. Have fun."

We watched her head for the front door then began our descent down the stairs.

"It's like she's got some sort of internal food sensor," I said, shaking my head.

"Yeah, if she's lost a step, I wouldn't have wanted to cross swords with her forty years ago," the Chief said.

"She's a sweet lady," Josie said, still fuming over her loss. "But if I smell chocolate on her breath in the morning, we're gonna have a problem."

Chapter 8

"How do you want to get started?" the Chief said, removing the soft plastic cover from the display terminal he was sitting in front of.

I sat down next to him and grabbed a folder that contained several laminated copies of a cross-referenced directory. Impressed with how the information was organized, I removed a roadmap from my pocket and unfolded it on the table directly behind our chairs.

"I thought we'd just use the north and south boundaries of the area Ms. McTavish has inputted and start with communities closest to the River," I said, pointing at the map to help clarify my strategy. "And if we don't find anything on that pass, then we'll just start moving inland."

"Sounds like a good plan," Josie said, nodding as she peered into the large screen and began getting used to the levers that moved the microfilm back and forth through the viewer. "Man, have we gotten spoiled."

"Tell me about it," the Chief said, laughing. "And I once thought that these things were a quantum leap forward in the technology."

"Just remember to cross off the towns on the map when you finish each search," I said. "Chief, why don't you take the north area, I'll do the center, and Josie can handle the south."

"How many nights do you think we're gonna be down here?" Josie said.

"Try not to think about it," I said, turning around in my chair to study the map.

"I'm hungry," she said.

"Try not to think about it," I repeated, now focused on the terminal in front of me. "Looking at this directory, I think using the list of school districts is the best way to make sure we cover all the towns."

"I think you might be right," the Chief said, glancing over my shoulder. "How do you want to handle the newspapers?"

"I think we should focus on the small weekly ones," I said. "They'd be more likely to run local stories about what was going on in the schools and churches. But don't forget the school yearbooks."

"Okay," Josie said, studying the directory. "Geez, there's a lot of small towns."

"Shhh," I said, concentrating on my viewer.

"Yes, Ms. McTavish," she said, laughing. "I think you might have missed your calling."

"Nah," I said, shaking my head. "I could never work in a place where you couldn't eat on the job."

"Excellent point."

We spent the next three hours in relative silence working our way through newspaper articles, columns, and hundreds of photos. Many of the microfilmed documents were blurry and hard to read, and about an hour in, I got a headache that soon turned relentless. But I was able to develop a review process that made my work more efficient, and I finally finished reviewing all of the newspapers then turned my attention to the microfilmed school yearbooks. Since the geographic area I was reviewing only contained seven school districts, I was able to get through the collection of yearbooks in just over an hour. I jotted down the missing years that Ms. McTavish hadn't gotten her hands on then tossed the pen down and stretched my arms over my head.

"Okay, I'm done with my first set," I said, getting up to cross off the communities on the roadmap.

"Any luck?" Josie said, not looking up from the screen.

"Nada," I said. "You?"

"Whatever luck I'm currently having is all bad," she said, sliding the lever to the next document.

"I got nothing," the Chief said, stifling a yawn. "What time is it?"

"Just past midnight," I said. "You want to call it a night?"

"Yeah, I think I can only handle one session a night," he said. "Same time tomorrow?"

"Maybe we can get started a bit earlier," I said.

"Right after dinner," Josie said, sliding the protective cover over the viewer. "Just so we aren't doing this on an empty stomach."

We said goodbye to the Chief then headed home to play with the dogs and grab a snack. I tried to finish the book I was reading but fell asleep and woke up with Chloe snoring at my feet and the book next to me. Deciding that I would have to wait to find out how Sherlock had solved the case, I headed for the shower then joined Josie and Chef Claire in the kitchen for breakfast. Josie had a scowl on her face and was toying with her omelet.

Josie being off her food was never a good sign.

"Good morning," I said, glancing back and forth at them. "What's going on?"

Josie looked across the island at Chef Claire and nodded.

"Tell her."

Chef Claire set her coffee down then shrugged.

"After your wedding, I'm thinking about taking a year off," she whispered.

"What?" I said, stunned. "Why would you do that?"

"I'm getting restless," she said, staring down at her coffee mug. "And I think my cooking skills are getting a little stale."

"*Your* cooking skills? You're joking, right?" I said.

"No, I'm not," she said, for some reason tearing up.

"What would you do?" I said.

"Travel," she said. "I have an idea for an international cookbook. But I need to do a whole bunch of research before I can write it."

"Research on what?" I said, helping myself to some of Josie's omelet.

"Regional cuisines, spices, cooking techniques," Chef Claire said, shrugging as she wiped her eyes with a napkin. "Why do I feel horrible about this?"

"Because you're upsetting the natural order of things," Josie deadpanned. "You know, modifying the balance and harmony we've worked so hard to build."

"Funny," Chef Claire said. "You're not helping."

"I'm still in shock," Josie said. "You're going to travel the world by yourself?"

"At the moment, it certainly looks that way," she said.

"That sounds way too dangerous these days, Chef Claire," I said. "What about Al and Dente?"

"I'd have to leave them here," she said. "But I don't know if I can handle being away from them for a year."

"I couldn't do that," Josie said, shaking her head.

"I know you couldn't," Chef Claire said. "Neither one of you could. But I'm seriously thinking about doing it. Does that make me a bad person?"

"No," I said, firmly. "It doesn't. And it goes without saying that the dogs can stay with us for as long as you need."

"Thank you," she whispered.

"How long have you been thinking about it?" I said.

"Quite a while. But I never had the money to do it the way I wanted," she said. "But then we sold Wags, and that problem went away in a hurry."

A few months ago, we'd sold our fledgling dog toy company for fifteen million, and Chef Claire's cut of three million would certainly make world travel a whole lot more comfortable.

"Good call on selling the company," Josie said, smacking me on the shoulder. "Next time you have a brilliant idea, keep it to yourself."

"Hey, you wanted to sell it too."

"But that was before I knew she was going to do something crazy like leave us," Josie said.

"I'm not leaving you," Chef Claire said. "I'm just taking a break. But you won't have to worry about the restaurants. Charlie's more than ready to take over C's here. And our place in Cayman runs like clockwork."

"Okay," I said, nodding absentmindedly as my mind began racing. "Wow, this is a lot to process."

"Are you in a hurry to get the cookbook out?" Josie said.

"Not really," Chef Claire said, shrugging. "It's just one of those projects I've been thinking about doing for a long time. Why do you ask?"

"Because if you'd be willing to spread it out over several trips of a month each, I can think of someone who'd be more than happy to travel with you," Josie said, finally focusing on her breakfast.

"Really? Who?" Chef Claire said.

"Me," Josie said, taking a bite of toast.

"You would?" Chef Claire said.

"Hey, that's not bad," I said, nodding.

"Now that's what a brilliant idea sounds like," Josie said, grinning at me. "And it would certainly help me avoid being the third wheel around you and Max for the next year."

"You'd never be the third wheel," I said.

"Aren't you sweet," Josie said.

"You're more like the appendix," I deadpanned.

"Funny."

"Wow," I said. "I can't imagine what it would be like around here without you two."

"I'm sure you and Max will come up a way to deal with it," Josie said.

"I'm sure we will," I said, laughing. "Still, I'm sure gonna miss you guys."

Josie took a big bite of her omelet then shrugged and smiled at me.

"Hey, it's not like we're running off to join the circus."

Chapter 9

At seven the next evening, we were back in the basement of the library picking up from where we'd left off. Our second search took us further inland from the River communities, but four hours later, we had again come up empty.

"I got nothing," Josie said, getting up to stretch. "I think we need a new plan, Snoopmeister."

"Yeah, this isn't working very well," I said. "But let's keep going. I think we can finish up with one more pass each."

"Okay, I'll do one more night," Josie said. "Let's get out of here."

"I think I'm going to stay and do some more," I said.

"Knock yourself out," she said, then glanced at Chief Abrams. "Can I get a ride home?"

"Sure," he said. "Maybe we can swing by C's for a nightcap."

"Perfect," Josie said, grabbing her bag and heading for the stairs. "Write if you get work."

"Yeah, I'll do that," I said, already studying Ms. McTavish's directory and comparing it to the roadmap on the table.

I sat down and began my third round of laborious research. I fought fatigue and forced myself to concentrate on what I was doing. Now dealing with communities located anywhere between thirty and fifty miles from the River, my confidence was fading fast, and the possibility that the Johnson family had been summer visitors and not year-round residents raised its ugly head. If that were the case, the family could have been from anywhere.

I had hoped to have a lot more background information on Samantha Johnson by the time the circus arrived, but I began contemplating a new strategy that would involve questioning as many performers as possible while they were in town. It was probably a good strategy for learning more about the dead woman, but definitely not a good approach for discovering who killed her. I was convinced her killer had to be someone from the circus. And my wandering around asking everyone in sight a ton of questions was bound to make people suspicious, especially the person who'd thrown her and the dog overboard.

Don't get me wrong. I was still planning on asking a lot of questions. But I wanted them to be queries that would take me forward and not wandering around in a circle.

And not get me killed in the process.

I focused on the screen in front of me, slid the lever to the right and the next image appeared on the screen. The headline grabbed my attention first: Bucks Bridge Man Commits Suicide. Underneath the headline was another written in smaller type: Sam Johnson, Professor, Dead at 46. Below that was a photograph of a farmhouse with two police cars parked in front along with an ambulance. I studied the photo then read the article.

Over the next fifteen minutes, I furiously scribbled in my notebook. Then I found Samantha's high school yearbook on microfilm. I walked to the long row of shelves on the other side of the basement and found the actual yearbook among the collection organized by year in alphabetical order.

"Ms. McTavish, bless your heart," I said, grabbing the yearbook. "You are so good."

I checked my watch and quickly packed up. I did my best lumber up the stairs and headed for the door. But I caught myself on the way out and opened the yearbook to the last page. I walked back to the front counter, added my name to the borrowing card, and left it on Ms. McTavish's chair. I locked the front door, set the alarm code, then walked to my SUV parked in front and made the two-minute drive to C's. I headed straight for the lounge and saw the Chief and Josie sitting at the bar chatting with Millie. All three frowned when they saw the look on my face.

"Let me guess," Josie said. "You saw a ghost."

"No, I found it," I said, nodding for them to follow me. I sat down on one of the couches and waited for them to get settled. I waved to Millie, and she held up a bottle of wine. I nodded to her then sat back and tried to catch my breath. "I can't believe it."

"I can't either," Josie said, taking a sip of her wine. "Are you sure it's her?"

"Positive," I said. "The family lived in Bucks Bridge."

"I have no idea where that is," Josie said.

"Sure, I know it. It's about five to ten miles outside of Potsdam," the Chief said. "It's tiny."

"Samantha's father was named Sam."

"Was?" Chief Abrams said, raising an eyebrow.

"Suicide," I said, glancing up when Millie arrived carrying a glass and a bottle of red. She poured mine and topped Josie's off. The Chief waved Millie's offer away. "Thanks, Millie. Do we have anything to snack on?"

"I'm sure I could find something in the kitchen," she said.

"No, don't bother," I said. "You've got customers to take care of."

"I could make some popcorn," she said.

"That would be great," I said. "I'm starving. Thanks."

Millie headed off, and Josie and the Chief focused on me.

"Suicide, huh?" the Chief said. "How did he do it?"

"He left his car running in the garage with the door closed. Waited until his wife and Samantha went to the movies one night, then grabbed a bottle of scotch and headed for the garage."

"Yuk," Josie said. "Why on earth did he do it?"

"Nobody knows," I said. "At least they didn't at the time. He didn't leave a note."

"What did he do for work?" the Chief said.

"He was a professor at Clarkson," I said.

Clarkson is a university in Potsdam well-known for its engineering programs as well as their hockey team that is often nationally ranked.

"How old was he when he died?" the Chief said.

I checked my notebook and tried to read my own writing.

"Forty-six. It was 1988."

"Thirty years ago," the Chief said. "How old was the girl when he died?"

I grabbed the high school yearbook from my bag and turned it to the page that displayed the girl's class photo. I passed it to the Chief.

"She was a sophomore," I said. "That would probably make her fifteen or sixteen."

"Well done," Josie said. "You didn't even need to count on your fingers."

I made a face at her then caught a whiff of fresh popcorn. My stomach rumbled, and I forced myself to focus. Chief Abrams handed the yearbook to Josie.

"Yeah, that's definitely her," Josie said, studying the photo. "She was a pretty girl."

"Which means that she could have also been forty-six when she died," the Chief said.

"You think that might be significant?" Josie said.

"I have no idea," the Chief said, shrugging. "But it is interesting. What was the wife's name?"

"Bella," I said. "Bella Johnson."

"She'd probably be somewhere in her seventies by now," the Chief said. "Assuming she's still alive."

"It shouldn't be hard to find out," I said. "Feel like taking a road trip tomorrow?"

"I'm booked solid tomorrow," Josie said.

"Tomorrow's my day off," the Chief said. "I was thinking about going fishing with Rooster."

"That's okay," I said, shrugging. "I'll just go by myself."

"Not a chance," the Chief said, shaking his head at me. "I'll tag along, but you owe me one."

"Only one?" Josie said.

"Yeah," the Chief said. "But my memory isn't what it used to be."

"You need to start writing them down," Josie said. "That's what I do."

Chapter 10

We headed northeast and followed the highway that provided gorgeous views of the River in several spots. When we reached Ogdensburg about an hour later, we headed south for a few miles before going east towards Potsdam on Route 11.

"Sorry to keep you from fishing," I said, glancing over at Chief Abrams in the passenger seat. "It's a great day to be out on the River."

"Don't worry about it," he said. "Oh, I almost forgot. I brought you a present." Then he caught the expectant look I was giving him. "No, it's not food."

He shook his head and removed a compact disc from his bag. He slid it into the player and moments later soft piano music filled the SUV.

"Nice," I said, nodding. "Keith Jarrett?"

"Well done. Koln concert. It's amazing. And since you've become quite the jazz fan, this one has to be part of your collection."

"I still can't believe how good some people get at what they do," I said, listening closely to the intricate solo piano. "It's a gift."

"Yes," the Chief said. "But even geniuses need to keep working to perfect their craft."

"Chef Claire just said the same thing," I said, then glanced over at him. "Not in those exact words, but that's what she was talking about."

"About her cooking?"

"Yeah," I said. "You know Chef Claire. She's too modest to use the word genius, but that's what she is."

"She is indeed," the Chief said. "She's worried she isn't working hard enough?"

"No, it's more like she's stopped learning," I said. "She wants to do a cookbook."

"I'd buy it," the Chief said, laughing. "That sounds like a fun project."

"She and Josie are going to start taking extended trips so Chef Claire can research regional cuisines."

"Really?" the Chief said. "How long?"

"Well, she was originally talking about taking a year off and going by herself."

"Traveling the world alone?" the Chief said. "Scary proposition these days." He pointed at an upcoming two-lane road. "Make a left."

"Yeah, we kinda freaked out when she mentioned it," I said. "That's when Josie offered to tag along if she was willing to take shorter trips."

"Good for them," he said, nodding. "How are you handling it? Change has never been your strong suit."

"I'll be fine," I said, shrugging. "Between the Inn, the new rescue center, and Max, I'll have more than enough to keep me busy."

"Where is Max at the moment?"

"Equador."

"Right, they had an earthquake. Hey, I've been meaning to ask you something. What are the new living arrangements going to be after the wedding?"

"Max is going to rent his place in Ottawa and move down here. And Josie is talking about buying the Bertram's place."

"Nice," the Chief said. "Just down the street, and she'll still be able to walk to work. And Chef Claire will be her roommate?"

"That's the plan," I said. "At least for now."

"Why do you say that?"

"It's just a feeling I have. Chef Claire seems really restless. And I'm not sure those trips are going to be enough to keep her happy."

"She's a big girl. And very smart. I'm sure she'll figure it all out."

"Yeah, I'm just being selfish," I said.

"Try not to beat yourself up too much," the Chief said.

"I'll try," I said. "Besides, Josie gets upset when I start cutting into her territory."

The Chief laughed then glanced out the window.

"Okay, this is the place," he said. "Bucks Bridge."

"Wow. I thought Clay Bay was small," I said, glancing outside at what appeared to be pretty much farmland. "It's pretty country. What body of water is that?"

"The Grasse River."

"Right," I said, nodding. "That's the one that comes out of the Adirondacks and dumps into the St. Lawrence near Massena."

"That's it. There's an old church here, but I don't think there's even a post office," the Chief said. "If I remember, the folks who live here have to pick up their mail a couple of miles up the road in Madrid."

"When were you here?"

"It was back when I was with the state police," he said. "I helped out on a case up here. Some genius thought he could move to a tiny hamlet and cook meth without anybody noticing."

"I take it people noticed," I said, laughing.

"Noticed the genius right into twelve years in federal prison," the Chief said.

"I take it he didn't work hard enough at perfecting his craft."

"To say the least," the Chief said, shaking his head at the memory.

"There's the farmhouse in the photo I saw," I said, slowing down. "How about that?"

"Judging from the flower beds, somebody is living here. Let's go have a look."

I pulled into the tiny driveway and parked right next to the house. It was small and needed a paint job but appeared to be reasonably well maintained. We climbed the short set of steps that led to the front porch and knocked. Seconds later, the door opened halfway, and an elderly woman poked her head out.

"Can I help you?" she said.

"Are you Bella Johnson?" I said with a smile.

"I am. Who are you?"

"I'm Suzy Chandler from Clay Bay. And this is Chief Abrams. He's our local police chief."

"Okay," she said, confused. "What do you want with me?"

"We're here about Samantha," I said.

The woman's eyes grew wide, and her mouth dropped. She let the door swing wide open but continued to stand in the doorway.

"Sammy? You have information about Sammy?"

"We do," I whispered.

"Please, come in," she said, stepping to one side and waving us in.

We entered and glanced around the small living room. Apart from the wallpaper that had a horrid flower pattern right out of the 1950s, the inside of the house was quaint and well-kept. Bella gestured for us to sit on the couch then sat down in a chair directly across from us and leaned forward.

"Please, tell me what you know," she said, her voice shaking.

I glanced at the Chief, and he stared back at me and eventually nodded.

"I hate to tell you this, Mrs. Johnson," the Chief said in a tone I knew he had perfected over the years delivering devastating news. "But we have some bad news to share with you. I'm afraid that Samantha drowned a few days ago in Clay Bay."

Bella Johnson stared at us in disbelief, then lowered her head and began sobbing. I got up and tried to comfort her, but she gently shook me off. I sat back down on the couch and waited patiently for her to find her bearings.

"What was she doing in the water?" she finally managed to get out. "Sammy was a terrible swimmer."

"Have you heard from her lately?" the Chief said.

"I got a letter a few weeks ago," she said. "Along with the check."

"Check?" the Chief said.

"She sent me a check about every three months," Bella said. "Usually, it was just the check. But the last one included a letter."

"Can I ask you what she said in the letter?" he said.

"Like usual, it didn't make a lot of sense," she said. "Just a bunch of rambling thoughts and run-on sentences. But she did say that she was going to try to visit me. She said she had a surprise."

"She didn't say what the surprise was?" I said.

"No," Bella said, starting another round of sobs. "I can't believe I was so close to seeing her again. And then this happens."

"How long has it been since you last saw her?" the Chief said.

"I haven't seen Sammy since she ran away," Bella said, appearing to be on the verge of hyperventilating. "That was thirty years ago."

I glanced at the Chief, but he was staring off into the distance deep in thought.

"I didn't hear a thing from her for over ten years, then the checks started showing up."

"You didn't try to track her down?" the Chief said.

"I tried everything. Cops, private investigators, you name it," she said, taking several deeps breath in rapid succession. "But nobody could find a trace of her. The postmarks were always from a different place."

"That makes sense," I said to the Chief. "The circus was constantly touring."

"Circus?" Bella said, staring at me.

"Samantha was a circus performer," I said.

"Really?" Bella said, giving me a wide-eyed stare.

"Yes. She had a trained dog act."

Bella sat back in her chair, and her head began to move as if it were a bobblehead doll moving in slow motion. Her eyes darted around the room, and she dug her nails into both knees.

For a moment, I thought we'd somehow been teleported into the middle of a poltergeist movie.

"I can't believe it," she said, shaking her head in anger. "You just couldn't stop mouthing off, could you? I hope you're happy."

The Chief and I both glanced around the room just to confirm there wasn't someone else in the room with us. She noticed our expressions then shrugged.

"I'm talking to him."

"Your ex-husband?" I said, cocking my head.

"Who else would I be talking to?"

"Well done," the Chief whispered.

"Lucky guess," I whispered back without taking my eyes off the woman whose agitation continued to ramp up.

"Always saying Sammy belonged in the circus," Bella said, her eyes continuing to dart around the room. "Just because she was a little bit different. I hope you're happy. You monster."

Both of us sat quietly and waited for her to snap out of whatever trance-like state she'd slipped into.

"Monster," Bella whispered, then began another round of sobs.

"Why do you think she never told you about working in the circus?" the Chief said.

"She probably couldn't bring herself to admitting that he was right," Bella said.

"He being your husband?" the Chief said.

"Who else would I be talking about?" she repeated.

Then she started doing the bobblehead thing again as she stared expectantly around the room.

"Okay," I whispered, leaning toward Chief Abrams who was closely watching the woman's movements. "I'm officially freaked out."

The Chief nodded without taking his eyes off her. Then he leaned forward and reached out and placed a hand on her arm. Bella flinched slightly, but her head stopped moving, and she focused on the Chief.

"Do you live here all by yourself, Mrs. Johnson?" the Chief said.

"I do. But Bobbie stops by to help me out," she said.

"Who's Bobbie?" the Chief said.

"He's a friend who lives up the road," she said. "He's been helping me for years. I just love what he's done with the garden this spring."

"It's very nice," I said. "How often does he stop by?"

"All the time," she said, staring out the window. "But I haven't seen him in a couple of days. And I'm running low on some things."

An idea floated to the surface, and I looked at the Chief who appeared to be thinking the same thing I was.

"We'd be happy to go to the store for you, Mrs. Johnson," the Chief said, removing his notebook from his pocket. "Just tell us what you need, and I'll make a list."

The Chief jotted a note on the page and held it out so I could read it. *Talk to Bobbie*. I nodded then leaned forward on the couch.

"Anything you need, Mrs. Johnson," I said. "We'll be happy to pick it up. Your mail, groceries, maybe your meds are running low."

"Don't start," the Chief whispered.

"I'm not starting anything," I whispered back. "She's scaring the crap out of me."

"No, that's quite all right. But thank you. I'm sure Bobbie will be here later today."

She sat back in her chair and calmly folded her hands on her lap.

"What were some of the things Sammy liked to do when she was young?" I said.

"Sammy didn't do a lot of things," Bella said with a sad smile. "But what she did do, she did a lot of."

"Okay," I said, repeating the odd statement silently in my head just to make sure I understood what she was saying. "What were they?"

"She loved playing with toy soldiers," Bella said, her eyes again drifting off as the memory washed over her. "No dolls for Sammy. She loved creating battles in her bedroom. Oh, the racket she made was enough to raise the dead." Bella returned to the moment and glanced back and forth at us. "And, of course, the dogs."

"Dogs?" I said. "You had dogs in the house?"

"Of course," she said, chuckling. "All the time. We used to breed them."

"You were a dog breeder?" the Chief said.

"For several years, yes," she said, then began sobbing again. "Right up until…my husband died. After that, I had to get rid of them."

"What breed?" the Chief said.

"Beagles," I blurted, then I felt my face turn red.

"How on earth did you know that?" Bella said, staring in disbelief at me.

I sat quietly, trying to decide if telling the old woman that the surprise her daughter had planned was to give her the Queens Beagle. I had no idea if telling her would lessen her pain or send off the cliff. Not willing to run the risk, I opted for a small lie.

"Just a lucky guess," I said, shrugging.

"Smooth," the Chief whispered.

"Shut it."

I smiled at her as she continued to stare at me. Then she looked out the window again.

"I wonder what's keeping him," Bella said. "Bobbie never goes more than a few days without stopping by."

"We'd be happy to swing by his place just to make sure he's okay," I said.

"I suppose that might be a good idea," she said. "He's just up the road."

"What's the address?" the Chief said.

"Oh, you don't need that," she said, waving it away. "You can't miss it. Turn right out of the driveway, and he's about a mile up on the left near the river. Yellow house with a big front porch. And you'll see his red truck in the driveway."

"Thank you," the Chief said, getting up from the couch. "We'll be going now. Thanks for your time. And we're so sorry for your loss. But I do need to ask you about the arrangements."

"Oh, my," Bella said, confused. "Sammy's body. Do you know where it is?"

"I do," the Chief said, handing her a business card. "This is the funeral home in Clay Bay. They have Samantha's body. Just give them a call, and they will be happy to discuss everything with you."

"Okay," she said as her head began to slowly move up and down, then side to side. "I really need Bobbie."

"We'll make sure he stops by as soon as possible," the Chief said.

"Thank you," she said, launching into a full-on bobblehead. "Are you happy?" she said in a violent whisper. "You monster."

"We'll show ourselves out," I said, grabbing the Chief by the sleeve and pulling him toward the door. "Again, we're so sorry for your loss, Mrs. Johnson."

"Look what you've done. Just look at what you've done," Bella whispered through clenched teeth. Her head continued its bizarre movements as she glanced around with a wild look in her eyes. "Monster. Coward. Monster. Coward."

I dragged Chief Abrams to the door and closed it behind us. We remained on the front porch and continued to hear her monster-coward chant grow louder until it reached a crescendo. Then I did my best lumber down the steps then climbed into the driver seat and waited impatiently for the Chief to get into the vehicle. I backed down the driveway, then headed in the direction of the yellow house.

"Slow down," the Chief said, reaching into his pocket for his notebook. "Here he comes."

A red truck was approaching from the other direction, and it slowed when it passed us. The driver gave us the once-over then pulled into the old woman's driveway. The Chief glanced over his shoulder, and when we were out of sight of the truck, he grabbed his phone and made a call.

"Hey, Tommy. Chief Abrams…Yeah, I'm good. Thanks. Look, I need you to run a tag for me."

The Chief recited the number of the truck's license plate then waited quietly, deep in thought.

"Robert Tompkins," the Chief said as he jotted the name down. "Yeah, a red F-150. That's the one…No, I don't need it right now, but if you could run the name and let me know if you get any hits, I'd appreciate it. Thanks, Tommy."

He put his phone away then turned up the volume on the Keith Jarrett CD that was still playing.

"Wow," the Chief said after a long pause. "I wonder if she's always like that, or if the news about her daughter just set her off."

"I'm gonna go with pretty much always," I said, checking for road signs that would take us back to Route 11. "Monster, coward. A monster because of how he treated her and Samantha?"

"That would be my guess," the Chief said.

"Coward because he killed himself."

"Yeah, that's gotta be it," the Chief said, nodding. "How on earth did you make the connection to the beagle?"

"It's just part of my ongoing efforts to perfect my craft," I deadpanned.

"Okay, Snoop," he said, laughing. "Man, that got spooky."

"Yeah, at one point I was expecting M. Night Shamalamadingdong to jump out from behind the couch and yell cut."

"Shyamalan," the Chief said.

"Yeah, I can never pronounce his last name," I said. "Shouldn't she be in some sort of institution?"

"I guess as long as she isn't hurting herself or anyone else, there isn't much anybody can do," he said. "And maybe Bobbie is really good with her."

"You're wondering if he might have been on that boat, aren't you?" I said, glancing over at him.

"The thought did cross my mind," the Chief said. "She said he hadn't been around to see her for a while."

"He joined the circus recently as some sort of hired hand, tossed Samantha and the dog off the boat, then quit and came home?" I said, frowning. "It's a bit of a stretch."

"It's a total stretch," he said. "And why would he do it?"

"Maybe she's leaving everything to him when she dies," I said. "And she showed him the letter all excited about Samantha showing up with a surprise."

"He panics about a possible mother-daughter reconciliation and decides to take Samantha out?" the Chief said. "Yeah, I suppose I can make that work."

"There's just one problem with it," I said. "If the mother has gone thirty years without knowing where her daughter was, how the heck did Bobbie find her?"

"Great question."

"Yeah, it's kinda the big one at the moment, isn't it?"

"What a weird day."

"And to think you were going to waste it fishing."

Chapter 11

I took a big bite of chocolate cake, ignored the disapproving glare I was getting from my mother, then gave Chef Claire two thumbs up. Josie took a sip of port, then reached for a second slice.

"Great call on using this port with the chocolate," Josie said to Chef Claire.

"Thanks," Chef Claire said, topping off everyone's glass. "But it's really not hard to figure that pairing out."

"Since I usually *pair* chocolate cake with a glass of milk, as always, your expertise astounds me," Josie said, raising her glass in salute. "I can't wait to see what you come up with after our trip to Italy."

My mother and I both looked at Josie.

"Oh, that's right," Josie said. "We haven't had a chance to update you yet."

"Update us on what?" my mother said.

"I'm going to do an international cookbook," Chef Claire said. "And Josie and I are going to start taking some time off to travel to places where I can study and research various regional cuisines."

"That sounds wonderful," my mother said, glancing at me to gauge my reaction. "And Italy is going to be your first trip?"

"It is," Chef Claire said. "We spent most of the day outlining our plan."

"I see," my mother said. "How long are you going to be away?"

"About a month each trip," Josie said.

"But not until after the wedding, right?" my mother said, raising an eyebrow.

"Don't worry, Mrs. C.," Josie said, laughing.

"If we didn't make the wedding, you'd kill both of us before we had a chance to get on the plane," Chef Claire said, laughing along.

"You got that right," my mother said. "So, when is this going to happen?"

"Well, my initial idea was to take a year off," Chef Claire said. "But when Josie offered to come with me, I decided to break it up. We're going to take two trips a year."

"Two?" I said, frowning. "Since when?"

"Since this afternoon," Chef Claire said. "We're looking at October after the season ends here. And since we spend most of our time in Cayman just kicking back, we thought we'd take a month out of that and make a second trip."

"You guys already have a schedule?" I said, finishing the last of my cake.

"I've had it done for quite a while," Chef Claire said. "We just needed to chunk it up today."

"Where else are you going?" my mother said, placing both elbows on the table and leaning forward.

"Let's see," Chef Claire said. "Italy in October, then Greece the following March. Year two is France and Spain. Then we'll start the Asian portion." She turned to Josie. "Do you remember the order we finally settled on?"

"Vietnam and Thailand. Then Japan and India. The year after that would be two trips to China."

"And that still won't be enough to really do it justice," Chef Claire said. "There are so many regional styles over there. We might also need a second trip to India."

"I'm sure we'll figure it out," Josie said. "And after that, Chef Claire wants to do Mexico and Peru."

"Wow," I said, feeling a tinge of envy. "That sounds amazing."

"And we'll be going to a bunch of cooking schools and classes," Chef Claire said, grinning. "I'm very excited."

I sat quietly sipping my port with my mind doing somersaults. Between the wedding, Samantha Johnson's murder, and the new rescue center, I was dealing with a lot. The fact that my two best friends would be on the road two months out of the year, not to mention the possibility that Max could be called away for weeks on end on a moment's notice, was starting to make me feel alone and vulnerable.

Even though I was excited about what I was dealing with and happy for Josie and Chef Claire, as much as I hated to admit it, my life was about to undergo several major changes that would be disruptive, potentially stressful and, in many cases, permanent. But I remembered Chief Abram's comment about my normal reaction to change and chastised myself again for my selfishness.

Deciding what was needed at the moment was another glass of port and a new topic of conversation, I refilled my glass and glanced over at my mother.

"How are the plans for the circus coming along?"

"Actually, quite well," my mother said. "Everyone on the council jumped on the idea right away. The logistics are done, and since the schools aren't out for the summer yet, we've been selling a lot of tickets through them at a discount. And Jackson is doing a promotion at his store. Two free tickets with every purchase of a hundred dollars of groceries. We just need to finish up with Chief Abrams on security and some street closure issues, and we'll be good to go."

"Crap," I whispered. I'd been hoping to get at least another week reprieve from the *dreaded binder.* I forced a smile at her. "Good for you, Mom. I knew you could pull it off."

"We have a lot of people working on it," she said, shrugging. "Where were you all day, darling? I tried calling three times, but your phone went straight to voicemail."

"I had it off most of the day," I said. "The Chief and I were visiting the tiny hamlet of Bucks Bridge."

My mother lowered the bite of cake she was about to eat and frowned as she stared off at the wall. Then she cocked her head and fixed her stare on me.

"It was that Johnson family?" she said.

"What are you talking about?" I said.

"The woman who drowned," my mother said, getting back to her cake. "She was originally from Bucks Bridge?" She slowly chewed then took a small sip of port. "Of course, Samantha. She was named after her father, wasn't she?"

"You're starting to freak me out, Mom," I said. "How on earth did you know that?"

"I remember the father's suicide," she said, giving me another shrug. "It was a major news story for days. I'm surprised Chief Abrams didn't remember it."

"I don't think he'd been transferred up here yet," I said.

"That's right," my mother said. "He didn't arrive until a few years after that. Her father was a professor, right?"

"Yes. At Clarkson," I said, then frowned. "Hey, wait a sec. Why would a suicide be a major story for days?"

"Because the police weren't convinced it was actually a suicide," she said, taking another bite of cake. "This truly is a remarkable dessert, Chef Claire."

"Thanks, Mrs. C."

"The cops thought he was murdered?" I said.

"As soon as they learned that the daughter had run away, I'm sure the thought crossed their minds."

"They suspected Samantha?"

"I think they suspected both of them at various points," my mother said. "Did you meet the mother today?"

"We did," I said, nodding.

"And?"

"It was…memorable," I said. "Mrs. Johnson is mentally unstable."

"Just unstable?" Josie said. "Or a total wingnut?"

"It was hard to tell," I said, shrugging. "The Chief and I had just told her that her daughter had drowned."

"Yeah, I can see where that would send a mother into orbit," Josie said. "The poor woman."

"But she was talking to the walls at different times. No, I take that back. Actually, she was talking to her dead husband," I said. "And she did this thing with her head that looked like something right out of The Exorcist."

"And you got the heck out of there just as fast as your little legs would carry you, right?" Josie said, laughing.

"Nothing gets past you," I said, laughing along. "She scared the crap out of me."

"I take it you didn't get any leads into who might have thrown her off the boat," Josie said.

"No, but Mrs. Johnson does have a guy who lives nearby who functions like her caretaker," I said. "There seemed to be something odd about that situation."

"Like what?" Josie said.

"I couldn't put my finger on it," I said, shaking my head.

"Because it was still shaking from watching the woman's head rotate?"

"You're on fire tonight," I said, grinning at her.

"Sugar rush," Josie said, draining the last of her port. "Oh, well. I'm sure you'll figure it all out once the circus comes to town."

"Darling, you made a promise to be on your best behavior," my mother said.

"Yeah, I hate when I do that," I whispered.

"What?"

"Nothing," I said, waving it off. "Don't worry, Mom. I won't be causing any public riots. And as long as we keep the clowns away from Josie, we should be in good shape."

"Funny," Josie said, then glanced at my mother's plate. "You gonna finish that, Mrs. C.?"

Chapter 12

To try and partially make up for ruining the Chief's day off, I invited him to have lunch with me at C's. I entered the restaurant through the kitchen, gave an obviously busy Chef Claire a quick wave then headed for the lounge. I leaned over the bar to give Millie a hug then sat down. I swiveled around in my stool and glanced around at the good-sized crowd.

"Busy," I said, nodding.

"The season is definitely starting to ramp up," Millie said. "Are you here for lunch?"

"Yeah, I'm meeting the Chief here. And Chef Claire said this morning that we definitely had to have the special."

"Good call," Millie said. "Then that means you're going to need a glass of this." She poured a large glass of iced tea and set it in front of me. "Say, we're interviewing for some summer bartenders this afternoon. You want to sit in?"

"Normally, I would," I said, stirring my tea. "But I don't think I can handle one more thing on my plate. Besides, between you and Chef Claire, you don't need me there."

"Are she and Josie really going to take all those trips?"

"Yeah, it certainly looks that way."

"I'm so jealous," Millie said. "I'd love to do something like that."

"I'm sure they wouldn't mind if you wanted to tag along on some of them," I said.

"Yeah, sure," Millie said, laughing. "Just as soon as I get my hands on several thousand dollars I don't need, I'll be all over that." Then she glanced past me and smiled. "Hey, Chief. How's it going?"

"Hi, Millie. It's certainly better than yesterday," he said, sliding onto the stool next to me. "Hey, Snoop. What looks good on the menu today?"

"Rhetorical, right?" I said. "You have to try the iced tea. And based on Chef Claire's recommendation, I'm going to go with the beef stew. With a side of cornbread."

"Perfect," he said as Millie poured then placed a glass of tea in front of him. He took a long sip and shook his head. "Even her iced tea is fantastic. What on earth is in this one?"

"I think this one is a black tea with cardamom and rosewater. And I'm picking up a touch of saffron."

"How does she come up with stuff like this?" he said, taking another sip.

"She's perfecting her craft, right?"

"I just throw some tea bags in a big jar and set it out in the sun," he said.

"And that's why you're a cop and not a chef," I said, laughing. "Were you able to track down the original case file?"

"I was. It's at the state police station in Ogdensburg," he said. "And I talked with one of the guys I used to work with."

"My mother remembers it," I said. "She said the cops suspected both the mother and daughter at one point."

"They did," the Chief said, staring at his glass of tea. "Who would come up with the idea of putting saffron in iced tea?"

"Focus, Chief," I said, patting his hand. "So, what happened?"

"The wife's alibi had a couple of holes in it, but it eventually held up."

"They went to the movies, right?"

"They did. And she had both ticket stubs," the Chief said. "But the wife really couldn't explain the plot of the movie."

"And the cops thought they went into the cinema then ducked out and killed him?"

"Yeah," the Chief said. "But after the cops interviewed her a few times, they understood why she might not remember the storyline."

"Why's that?" I said, glancing over at him.

"You saw her yesterday. What do you think?"

"So, she's always been like that?" I said.

"Apparently," the Chief said. "And the state and local cops had been out to the house several times. She was always calling to report intruders or people she felt were doing surveillance on her."

"Did any of them ever check out?"

"No," the Chief said. "In fact, the night she called to report the suicide, they didn't believe her at first."

"And they never got a chance to question the daughter?"

"They did not," he said, sliding his glass forward for a refill. "Eventually, they quit looking for the girl and decided to close the case as a suicide."

"I wonder how Samantha managed to pull off her disappearing act."

"It's not that hard," the Chief said. "Especially if you don't want to be found. A couple million kids run away from home every year in this country."

"But in a small town like that, she must have had some help, right?"

"Not really," he said, shaking his head. "Get to the highway and hitch a ride with a trucker. There'd be a lot of people who'd stop to pick up a cute teenage girl. Especially thirty years ago. By the next morning, she could have been five hundred miles away in any direction."

"But she had to leave her dogs behind," I said. "Bella said her daughter loved spending time with them."

"Which probably tells us just how bad the family situation must have been, right?"

"Yeah, but still. I could never do that."

"I know you couldn't," he said, squeezing my hand then sitting back to give Millie room to set our lunch down in front of us on the bar. "Thanks, Millie."

"You're welcome," she said, topping off our iced tea. "I tried some of the stew earlier. You're not gonna believe it."

"New recipe?" I said, suddenly on point.

"Yeah," Millie said. "She wouldn't tell me what she's added to it."

I took a bite, savored it, then took another. Chief Abrams did the same then looked at me.

"I have no idea what she did to it," he said. "But it's fantastic."

"Total knee-buckler," I said, grinning at him as I broke off a piece of cornbread. "It's Moroccan."

"And you know this how?" the Chief said, taking another bite of the stew.

"Horrible syntax, Chief."

"Don't start."

"The spice blend is Ras el Hanout," I said. "It's used in a lot of North African dishes. It's similar to Garam Masala that's used in Indian cooking. There are hundreds of variations, but this one seems to have an extra dash of cardamom."

"Cardamom? She made a conscious choice to pair the stew with the iced tea?" he said, frowning.

"I'm sure she did," I said, shrugging as I rapidly worked my way through the bowl of stew. "Attention to detail, right?"

"I'm picking up a bit of sweetness," he said. "Is that coming from the spices?"

"No, the spice blend is what's giving it the overall flavor and heat," I said.

"Then it must be honey."

"No. Figs."

"Figs? Well, they certainly work," the Chief said. "The chickpeas are a nice touch."

"They are," I said, forcing myself to slow down.

"I can't believe she's worried that her skills are slipping."

"Yeah," I said. "Just think about how good she's going to be when she gets back from her trips."

"She'll be a rock star," the Chief said, dipping his cornbread into the gravy.

"She's already a rock star," I said. "I wouldn't even know how to describe her when she gets back." Then I felt a wave of emotion surge through me. "If she comes back," I whispered.

"You're really worried she might not?"

"No, I'm not worried," I said, shaking my head. "It's just that I know this phase of my life is about to end."

"Just when you finally get it perfected, right?" he said, laughing.

"Yeah. Something like that."

"Well, then you're just going to have to start working on perfecting your new craft, aren't you?"

"And what would that be?" I said, confused.

"Why, wife and mother, what else?"

"You know something, Chief? That's a very good way of looking at it. I like that."

"You're gonna be great at both," he said, patting my hand.

"There you are."

We both turned around when we heard my mother's voice.

"I've been looking everywhere for you, darling."

"Hi, Mom," I said, giving her a hug. "You want some lunch?"

"Maybe in a bit," she said, sitting down next to me and placing the dreaded binder on the bar. "But before I do, we really need to make a decision about which invitations we're going to go with." She flipped the pages, landed on one, then turned to me. "Personally, I like this design. But the sample I have is the wrong color of white."

"Wrong white," I said, nodding. "Got it."

"I'm glad you see it too," my mother said, turning to another page. "This is the white I think we should go with. And if we use that design with this shade of white, I think we'll have something very special."

"Sure, sure," I said, watching as she flipped back and forth between the two pages. I looked at the Chief who was shaking his head as he watched us. "I can't start trying to perfect my new craft until after the wedding, right?"

"Probably not," he said, laughing.

"Crap."

Chapter 13

Based on the strength of ticket sales, aided by what I was sure was my mother's anonymous donation of several hundred tickets to organizations that worked with underprivileged children and low-income families, a second performance was added to accommodate the number of people who were coming to the circus. The fact that I would have close to three days to do some serious snooping took some of the pressure off and definitely helped my mood that had been hovering between nervous and sullen for the past several days.

"What a mess," Josie said, staring out at the acreage behind the Inn that had been transformed into a construction zone.

"You're being kind," I said, glancing around at the earthmoving equipment and stacks of steel pipe and cinder blocks along with various other building materials. A group of workers and several welders were building numerous cages of various sizes and making one heck of a racket. "We must be nuts."

"I blame your mother."

"Me too," I said. "You want to walk down and take a closer look?"

"No, I think I'd rather wait until they get a bit further along," she said. "And we don't want to run the risk of you getting run over by a bulldozer."

"Good call. I have been a bit distracted lately," I said, heading back toward the Inn.

"Sì, hai, amico mio," Josie said, enunciating each word slowly. Then she beamed at me. "That translates into yes, you have, my friend."

"You're working on your Italian already?"

"It's never too early to start, right?" she said, gently punching me on the shoulder. "Are you going to be okay with all these changes?"

"I think I am," I said, glancing over at her as we headed across the empty play area. "I had a nice chat with the Chief that helped my perspective."

"He's a wise man," she said. "You want to do a fridge clean tonight and watch a movie?"

"Sure, if we can eat early," I said, holding the back door open for her. "But I'm going to have to pass on the movie."

"You got other plans?"

"I do," I said, following her inside. "The circus is coming to town."

"You're going to go watch them set up?" Josie said.

"Among other things," I said. "You want to come with me? I doubt if the clowns will be in costume tonight."

"Funny," she said. "No, thanks. I'll pass. I have some research to do I might as well get started on."

"Like what?"

"Well, I need to check out the cooking school that we're going to."

"You're going to go to cooking school with her?" I said, opening the back door that led to the dog condos.

"I thought I might," Josie said. "I'd love to learn how to do some of the things she does."

"When in Rome, right?" I said, shrugging.

"Actually, I think we're going to be out in the country," Josie deadpanned.

"Maybe I won't miss you so much after all."

"Yeah, right," Josie said, making a face at me. "And I want to see if there are any rescue centers or vets in the area. I'll need a way to get my dog fix while I'm gone. You sure you don't mind taking care of Captain?"

"Well, it's a lot to ask, but I think I can manage," I said, laughing.

"Going away for a month," she said, shaking her head. "He's never going to forgive me."

"Oh, I'm sure he'll forgive you," I said. "Eventually."

We entered the registration area and found Jill sitting at the computer with the beagle on top of the counter watching her closely. The dog stood and wagged its tail when she saw us.

"Hey, Queen B.," I said, gently scratching the dog's ear. "You seem happy today."

"She is," Jill said, rolling her chair back and patting her lap.

The beagle hopped down off the counter onto the desk, then onto Jill's lap. The dog placed its front paws on her shoulders and licked her face. Jill beamed at us as she stroked the beagle's back.

"I just love her so much," Jill said.

"Yes, we've noticed," Josie said.

"So, what do you think about the idea of Sammy and me adopting her?" Jill said.

"We love the idea," I said. "But I wouldn't feel right if we didn't check with the circus people first to see if Queen B. is somehow connected to somebody there."

"Okay," Jill said, frowning.

"I hate to do it, Jill," I said. "But how would you feel if you lost Tripod?"

Tripod was their three-legged Cocker Spaniel they'd adopted from a litter Josie and I had rescued from an illegal puppy mill that had been operating in the area. One of the dog's front legs had gotten frostbite, and Josie had performed the surgery to remove it. But the Cocker had quickly adapted to the loss of the leg, and if the dog now somehow fit society's definition of handicapped, Tripod sure didn't know it.

"Yeah, I get that," Jill said, hugging the beagle. "What about the woman's mother?"

"What about her?" I said.

"You said that the daughter was probably planning on giving Queen B. to her," Jill said.

"Yes, I think that was her plan," I said. Then I flashed back to Bella Johnson's rotating head and her rants at her dead husband. "But I don't think that would be good for the dog. And you know our motto."

"Whatever's best for the dogs," Jill said, nodding.

"Exactly," I said. "And I don't know how much longer Mrs. Johnson is going to be able to live by herself in that house. She seems to be slipping away, and the news about her daughter certainly didn't help. It wouldn't be a good place for Queen B. I'll let you and Sammy know as soon as I can."

"Thanks, Suzy," Jill said, setting the beagle on top of the counter.

The dog cocked its head at us and seemed to be studying us closely.

"You really are an inquisitive little girl, aren't you?" Josie said, reaching out to accept the paw Queen B. was holding out. "Maybe we should just let you decide where you want to live."

"Now, there's an idea," I said, laughing. "What do you say, Queen B.? You want to go back to the circus, or would you rather stay here with Jill and Sammy?"

The dog hopped down off the counter and back onto Jill's lap. Then she looked at us before nuzzling Jill's neck and rolling over on her back.

"There you go," Josie said. "Question asked and answered."

Chapter 14

I parked on the street and followed the floodlights into the public park near the water where the main circus tent was already up. I hung back and surveyed the scene of a couple of dozen workers scurrying around doing a wide variety of tasks. I recognized several of them as performers we'd watched in Brockville, and it was impossible to miss how hard they were working. When I spotted Mr. Pontilly standing near one of the floodlights studying a document, I headed his way.

"Claude," the old man called out. "I think we should move it about ten feet to the left."

I looked at Master Claude, the animal trainer I'd used the cattle prod on, who was dressed down in jeans and a tee shirt. He followed the old man's instruction then began pounding a large stake into the ground.

"Hello, Mr. Pontilly," I said as I approached. "Welcome to Clay Bay."

He turned around, recognized my face immediately, then held up a finger.

"Hang on," he said. "Don't tell me. I'll get it. You're the one with the contract who has problems with animal acts. Hang on, it'll come to me." He concentrated hard with a frown on his face. "Brockville. Hang on. Suzy. Right?"

"Well done," I said, grinning. "It's nice to see you again. Is there anything you or your folks need?"

"No, I believe we're all set," he said, glancing around. "Your mother stopped by earlier and helped us get settled in."

Good, I thought. She'll be off the wedding plans for the next few days.

"She's a remarkable woman," he said. "Incredibly organized."

"Yeah, she's a whiz with a binder," I said, shrugging.

"What?"

"Nothing," I said, glancing around. "This looks like a lot of work."

"It's what we do," he said, looking around with pride. "Come to town, set it up, do the show, take it down, move on to the next stop." He nodded to himself, pleased with his summary description of circus life. "Actually, using the boat on this tour is making our job a lot easier."

"So, Samantha's idea was good?"

"Very much so," he whispered. "That poor girl. Tragic."

"How long did she work for you?"

"Oh, my, let me think for a moment," he said. "Probably close to twenty-five years."

"Twenty-five?" I said, immediately wondering how Samantha had spent the first five years after she'd run away. "That's a long time."

"Not when you've been doing it for over sixty," he said, laughing.

"Fair point," I said, smiling at him. "Where did you originally find her? I mean, dog acts can't be that common."

"Actually, the dog act came much later. At first, she was just a hired hand. You know, helping out setting up and breaking things down after the show. A jack of all trades sort of thing. And then she started helping Claude out with the animals. Over time, she came up with the idea of the dog act, and we eventually added it."

"What's going to happen with the dog act now that she's gone?" I said, doing my best to push the conversation in the direction I wanted without making him suspicious.

"Her assistant is taking it over," he said. "In fact, tomorrow night will be her first performance with the dogs. She's been working very hard to get up to speed."

"How many dogs are in the act?" I said.

"I believe it's ten," he said. "No, I take that back. It's nine. The other dog wasn't in the show."

Bingo.

I seized the opportunity to chat about the beagle.

"Other dog?" I said, going for casual.

"Sam's personal dog," he said. "It was a toy beagle that she had gotten somewhere during one of our tours."

"The poor dog," I said. "I'm sure it's missing her."

"No, I'm afraid the dog is gone. We think it must have gone overboard with Sam when she went into the water."

"Maybe the dog will turn up," I said. "Their resilience and survival instincts can be surprising at times."

"I suppose you're right," he said as he looked out at the River and shook his head. "I still can't believe she's gone."

A man wearing shorts and a tee shirt approached. A cigarette was hanging out of his mouth, and he was looking down at the ground deep in thought. Then he looked up and grinned when he saw me.

"Hey, look who's here," he said.

I didn't recognize the face, but I remembered the voice.

"Hey, Chuckles. Right?" I said, grinning at the clown.

"That's me," he said, nodding.

"I didn't recognize you out of costume," I said.

"That's one of the reasons I love being a clown," he said. "Nobody ever knows who I am. Thanks again for the two hundred bucks."

"Don't mention it. It was worth every penny."

Mr. Pontilly didn't have a clue what we were talking about, and he glanced back and forth at us.

"She paid Bubs and me to have some fun with her friend at a recent show," Chuckles said.

"Let me guess," the old man said. "Another clown-phobic."

"Yeah," Chuckles said. "I thought she was going to wet her pants." Then he focused on me. "Is she coming to the show tomorrow night?"

"I think there's a good chance," I said, nodding.

"Well, just let me know if you need our services."

"I'll do that," I said, laughing.

"Mr. Pontilly, I need to have a chat with you if you have a few minutes," Chuckles said, then glanced at me.

I got his silent message to get lost and looked at the old man.

"Would it be okay if I took a look around, Mr. Pontilly? I've never seen a circus being set-up for a performance before."

"Of course," he said. "But please be careful and pay attention to what you're doing. There are a lot of moving parts going on at the moment."

"I'll do that. Thanks," I said. "I'll see you tomorrow, Chuckles."

I headed for the tent and stepped inside. One of the aerialists I remembered from the performance in Brockville was watching another man put the finishing touches on the netting they used during their act. Then I glanced up and noticed a woman swinging back and forth on a trapeze near the top of the tent.

"Okay, we're all set," a man holding a wrench called out. "Ready when you are, Wanda."

"Got it," the woman called back.

She began swinging faster on the trapeze and made several passes back and forth across the tent. My stomach began to churn as I watched her speed increase with each one. Halfway across on her final pass, she released the bar and launched herself into the air, did a triple-somersault then dropped like a rock. She landed on the net, bounced a few times then expertly grabbed the edge of the net with both hands and flipped herself over and stuck the landing. She wiped her hands on a towel and nodded.

"That's perfect, Jim," she said to the man holding the wrench. "I'll meet you guys at the restaurant around nine." Then she did several backflips across the tent and eventually disappeared from sight.

"Nimble little thing," I said out loud to myself.

I followed the direction her backflips had taken her and soon found myself in the same area I'd been in before in Brockville. I walked past several workers who barely acknowledged my presence, and I passed the wardrobe room where a man was digging through boxes of makeup. A woman was also in the room organizing costumes on metal racks on wheels. I continued my stroll and soon found myself outside again and heard the trumpet of an elephant. On my way toward the gigantic animal, I passed Master Claude who was staring back and forth at two cages that contained tigers. He glanced up when he heard my approach and stared at me.

"Can I help you?" he said.

"No, I'm just having a look around," I said, doing my best not to punch him. "Mr. Pontilly said it was okay."

"All right," he said, giving me an admiring once-over. "I'd be happy to give you a tour."

"That sounds good," I said, biting my bottom lip. "I'd love to see the elephant."

"Sure, why not?" he said, wiping the sweat from his face. "Follow me."

I did.

At a safe distance.

Soon, we were standing next to a temporary metal barrier that was about three feet high and no more than fifteen feet across. I'd find the space confining. I couldn't imagine how the elephant that had to weigh over a couple of ton felt about the size of his home. One of the elephant's legs was chained to a metal post, and I felt my blood begin to boil.

"This is Beulah," Master Claude said.

"She's gorgeous," I said, taking a step closer.

"Careful. Don't get too close," he said, placing a hand on my arm.

"I'll be fine," I said, taking a couple of steps forward until he had to let go.

The elephant paused from its snack of a bale of hay and made eye contact with me. It held out its trunk, and I reached out and stroked it. The skin reminded me of leather that had gotten wet then dried rough and wrinkled. The elephant continued to stare at me then lifted its trunk and gently placed it on my shoulder.

"That's amazing," Master Claude said. "She hasn't done that with me in years."

"Stop jabbing hooks in her," I whispered.

"What?"

"I said, just look at her. She's so beautiful," I said, then glanced underneath the elephant. "I'm assuming it's a she."

"She is. You're good with animals."

"I have my moments," I said, continuing to stroke the elephant's trunk. "Beulah. What a good girl." I glanced at Master Claude. "You know, I was at your recent performance in Brockville and noticed she didn't perform that night."

"Yeah," he said, staring off. "I was out of commission that night."

"Really? What happened?" I said, going for coy.

"Back spasms," he said with a shrug.

"I bet," I whispered to the elephant, then turned to him. "I hate when that happens. Back spasms are the worst."

"Yeah, no argument from me," he said, then brightened. "Say, a bunch of us are going to dinner in a while. Why don't you join us?"

"Where are you going?"

"Some restaurant called C's," he said. "You familiar with it?"

"Actually, I'm one of the owners," I said, slowly reeling my line in. "That sounds great, Claude. What time should I meet you there?"

"We're going around nine," he said, again placing a hand on my arm. "I'm looking forward to it. At least I am now. And after that, maybe you can show me around town. We can get to know each other a bit better."

I almost threw up in my mouth, but I opted for casually flashing my engagement ring in his direction. He glanced at it, then shrugged it off.

"Or maybe we can grab a bottle of wine and just sit and talk. You know, some secluded place near the water."

"One never knows, Claude," I said, forcing a smile at him. "Okay, Beulah. You be a good girl."

I gently stroked her trunk, then the elephant trumpeted loudly and draped the trunk over my shoulder again.

I took it that she was either protesting the fact I was leaving or warning me to stay away from Master Claude.

Or maybe a bit of both.

Chapter 15

The group of circus performers around the table, as you might expect, was an interesting collection of characters. Apart from their love of living the circus life, after an hour, it appeared that their only other shared interest was a fondness for alcohol. Mr. Pontilly was holding court at the head of the table and regaling the group with stories about circus life I was sure they'd all heard dozens of times. But since the stories were new to me, I found them fascinating except for those that dealt with the acquisition, training, and treatment of the various wild animals he had used in his circus over the years. During those stories, I tuned out and did my best not to listen by creating a mental checklist of all the things I needed to get done and humming show tunes.

I was sitting next to the old man who was using his hands to punctuate his stories, often with a glass of wine in his hand. As such, I was in the splash zone, and my white blouse was beginning to look like I'd been shot in several places. But I hung tough since I had a feeling that the person who had thrown Samantha Johnson off the boat was either sitting at the table or that one or more of the diners knew who did.

Sitting on the other side of me was a woman who went by the name of Grundella.

Yeah, I know. I frowned and almost laughed when I heard it the first time, too.

Grundella, bottle-blonde and somewhere around a hard-thirty, had formerly been Samantha's assistant and now ran the dog act. But rather than coming across as a dog person, she gave me the impression that the dogs were more of a way to make a living rather than having a genuine desire to spend most of her time around our four-legged friends. She was nice enough, but rough around the edges and was flirting back with Master Claude who was sitting at the other end of the table and casting furtive glances in our direction. I was pretty sure I was the target of Master Claude's intense stares but made no effort to enlighten her, and halfway through the salad course, her breathing had turned shallow. The more I continued to ignore the animal trainer, the more he intensified his stares, and Grundella groaned and almost fell out of her chair at one point. But to be fair, I must confess that Master Claude's efforts at *haunting glances* also began to work their magic on me.

I was certain I'd be haunted right into several nightmares over the coming days.

Next to Grundella was the aerialist I'd seen earlier in the tent and her brother, Miguel. The woman was named Wanda, and when she shook hands with me, it was like I had stuck my hand in a vise lined with sandpaper. I caught a glimpse of the calluses on her hands and was impressed when I realized the thousands of hours of practice it must had taken to create them.

And if she and her brother had an ounce of body fat on them, I had no idea where they were hiding it.

Sitting on either side of Master Claude were Bubs and Chuckles, the two clowns who'd terrified Josie in Brockville. When I finally got a good look at them in bright light, I realized they had to be close to sixty. Their faces were roadmap-wrinkled, and both had chronic, phlegmy coughs I chalked up to years of heavy smoking.

I finished my salad, took a sip of water, then launched.

"Tell me about your dog act," I said.

When Grundella didn't respond, I nudged her gently with an elbow and sat waiting for her to focus on me. She tore her eyes away from Master Claude and looked over.

"Oh, it's not bad," she said with a shrug. "Actually, I'm a little nervous. Tomorrow night is my first performance."

"How long were you Samantha's assistant?" I said, starting her off with an easy one.

"About three years," she said, reaching for her wine and sneaking in a quick glance down the table.

"Pardon my nosiness," I said, following her eyes down the table. "But do the two of you have something going on? He can't take his eyes off you."

"Yeah, I know," she whispered. "It's weird. I've been trying to get another shot at him for months, but he's never shown any interest. All of a sudden, it's like he can't wait to get to me alone."

"Men, huh?"

"Yeah," she said, laughing. "But just between you and me, he can *tame* me anytime he wants."

Okay. So much for Grundella's taste in men.

"I wish you luck," I said, refilling her wine glass.

"I'm probably gonna need it," she said. "Like Sammy used to say, Claude can be very *demanding*."

"Really? They were an item?"

"For a while," Grundella said, taking a slug of wine. "Then Claude dumped her."

"Why did he do that?" I said, leaning in a bit.

"Sammy could be a little…"

"Demanding?"

"No," Grundella said, shaking her head.

"Jealous?"

"Sometimes," she said. "But mostly Sammy was just freaking nuts."

"Really?" I said, remembering my time with the dead woman's mother.

"Cuckoo for Cocoa Puffs," Grundella said, taking another big slug of wine.

I refilled her wine then took a small sip of mine.

"Yeah, Claude was lucky to escape her clutches," Grundella said.

"She should've used the cattle prod," I whispered as I glanced down the table.

"What?"

"Nothing," I said, shaking my head. "So, Sammy was unstable?"

"That's a word for it," she said. "Especially when she was off her meds. The only thing that seemed to calm her down were the dogs. Especially that beagle."

"She had a beagle?" I said, going for casual.

"Queen B.," Grundella said, gulping down half her wine.

I refilled her glass.

As long as she kept talking, I was going to keep pouring.

"Where's the dog now?" I said.

"My guess is somewhere at the bottom of the river," she said. "We didn't find the dog anywhere, so she must have had it with her when she jumped off the boat."

I studied her closely and didn't pick up a trace of a lie.

"Suicide, huh?"

"Yeah, just like her old man," Grundella said.

"Really? Her father?"

"Yup," she said, tossing back half her glass.

"How did he do it?" I said.

"She never said. Sammy was what I called half a storyteller. Especially that one. Every time the conversation turned to family, she'd start ranting and raving, then bawl and take off somewhere to be alone," Grundella said, glancing over at me. "Like I said, cuckoo for Cocoa Puffs."

"She must have had a tough childhood," I said.

Grundella laughed then downed what was left in her glass.

"Yeah, that must have been it."

"I'm not following," I said, pouring what was left of the bottle into her glass.

"We've *all* had crappy childhoods," she said. "It's number one on the list of requirements to work in the circus."

"How did you end up working for Mr. Pontilly?"

"I was one of his rescues," Grundella said.

"I beg your pardon?"

"Apart from the aerialists and a couple of the specialty acts, we're all rescues. You know, members of the Pontilly *family*," she said, now officially buzzed.

I knew I was probably taking advantage of her current condition, but the rescue comment stuck with me and was already beginning to nag.

"You do know what a rescue is, right?" she said, glancing over at me.

"Yeah, I could probably ballpark it."

"That's us," she said, scowling. "Mutt-central."

"Where were you rescued from?" I said, reaching for one of the fresh bottles of Pinot our server had placed on the table.

"He found me sleeping in a bus station outside of Chicago," Grundella said.

"Homeless?" I said as a wave of sympathy surfaced.

"No, most nights I was able to find someone to go home with," she said, making eye contact. "If you catch my drift."

"Got it," I said. "How old were you?"

"Sixteen, by then," she said. "I took off at fourteen."

"And your parents never found you?" I said.

"I doubt they ever looked," Grundella said, then cut loose with a wicked laugh. "Except for maybe behind the couch. But even that was probably too much work for them."

"That's so sad," I whispered.

"Hey, we all got our sad stories, right?" she said, shrugging.

"Yeah, I guess," I whispered as my guilt about my own privileged life again raised its ugly head.

"Yes, the Pontilly family is quite the collection," Grundella said, toying with her wine glass. "We got all kinds here. Ex-hookers, dealers, thieves and grifters, you name it. Coming soon to your town under the big top." She took another big gulp then exhaled loudly.

"Where did Mr. Pontilly find Samantha?" I said, taking a sip.

"The same place as he found the rest of us," she said. "On the street. He found Sammy in Omaha."

"I wonder how she ended up in Omaha," I said more to myself than her.

"I think you turn left at Sioux Falls," she deadpanned, then grinned at me. "Pontilly found Claude outside of San Diego. And he found the two clowns when they were working some con job at the Idaho state fair. Actually, he ended up bailing them out after they got arrested."

"And the aerialists?" I said, nodding at the brother and sister team who were chatting with Mr. Pontilly who'd pulled up a chair between them.

"The Princess and the Silent One?" Grundella said, finally taking a bite of her salad. "Pontilly actually recruited them from another circus."

"I've seen them perform," I said. "They're very good."

"They work hard at their craft," she said. "I have to give them that."

"I take it you're not fond of them."

"Not much," she said. "They don't have a lot of time for us *rescues*. No, I take that back. They did like Sammy."

"Interesting," I said, studying the woman named Wanda who appeared to be getting agitated by her conversation with Pontilly. "Why do you think Samantha jumped off the boat?"

"Well, that seems to be the million-dollar question, doesn't it?" Grundella said. "I have no idea. And it happened at such a weird time. She was really excited about the summer tour."

"Do you know why?"

"No, Sammy wouldn't talk about it," she said. "I guess the reason she went in the water is going to remain a mystery."

"Oh, I hate when that happens."

"Yeah," she said, polishing off the last of her wine. "Loose ends are never fun."

"I agree," I said, sitting back in my chair. "I can't help but wonder why she did it."

"Maybe she didn't jump," Grundella said, making eye contact.

"Do you think that's a possibility?" I said, doing my best to sound casual.

"Hey, it's the circus," she said. "Anything's possible. Now, if you'll excuse me, I think I'll use this wave of liquid courage to my advantage."

"What?"

"I'm going to go chat up Claude before my buzz wears off."

Chapter 16

The next night we took two cars to the performance. I was driving my SUV with Josie in the passenger seat, and Chef Claire was in the back seat with Sammy and Jill. I followed my mother who had Paulie and Rooster in the car with her. I parked on the street right behind her, and we briefly huddled as a group while my mother handed us our tickets. Then she gave me a quick once-over and nodded her approval at my outfit.

"You look very nice tonight, darling."

"Thanks, Mom. You too."

I draped an arm over her shoulder as we strolled along the path that led to the main tent.

"Remind me to discuss your honeymoon wardrobe with you," she said. "I have a few suggestions."

"I'd be shocked if you didn't, Mom."

Just inside the enormous tent that was almost filled to capacity, Chief Abrams was chatting with a small group of security guards who'd been hired to help out with the event. He finished giving them a set of instructions, then watched as they headed off to their assigned areas.

"Hey," the Chief said when he spotted us. "We're all going to be on our best behavior tonight and just enjoy the show, right?" he said to the group, but staring at me.

"Geez, have a little faith, Chief," I said.

"Trust me," he said. "I've been praying every night."

"You're really not as funny as you think you are," I snapped.

"Disagree," Josie and Chef Claire said in unison.

"We're sitting in the front row on the left, Chief," my mother said, laughing. "If you hear a ruckus, you might want to check that area out first."

I scowled, bit my bottom lip, but said nothing as I waited out the laughter.

"Ooh, funnel cakes," Josie said, eyeing the row of food vendors. "Maybe I'll actually get one this time."

"Not if I find the clowns first," I said with a grin.

"Funny," Josie said, making a face at me. "Just try not to shoot anybody tonight."

"Hey, I'm not making any promises," I said.

I made a mental note of where we were sitting then started to head for the area where the performers were getting ready behind the set of curtains.

"Where on earth are you going?" my mother said.

"I just need to have a quick chat with someone, Mom," I said.

"Suzy, if you send those clowns over here, I swear I'm gonna kill you," Josie said.

"Harsh," I said, grinning at her. "Relax. Trust me, I promise you that I won't be giving the clowns any money tonight to terrorize you."

"Thank you," Josie said, nodding her head once. "C'mon, Chef Claire. Let's go grab some funnel cakes." She pointed at the area where the food vendors were lined up in a long row. "Ooh, corn dogs."

I watched them head off with a big grin on my face. Then my mother sidled up next to me.

"You're not going to give the clowns any money *tonight*?" she said, with a coy smile.

"Absolutely not," I said, shaking my head. "I'm a woman of my word."

"You gave it to them last night during dinner, didn't you?"

"Nothing gets past you, Mom," I said, laughing as I gave her a hug. "I'll be right back."

"Please try not to annoy anyone, darling."

"Sure, sure."

I approached the same guy I'd seen in Brockville standing guard outside the entrance to the performer area. Instead of the lime green tuxedo he'd been wearing the first time I saw him, the one tonight was a blinding canary-yellow.

"Hey, it's good to see you again," I said. "Nice tux. Banana Republic, right?"

"Don't start," he said, frowning at me.

"Suddenly, I'm in the mood for a piece of fruit," I said, laughing.

"Yeah, good one. You need to speak with somebody back there?"

"I need to have a quick word with Wanda," I said.

He stared at me briefly, then nodded and started to pull the curtains apart.

"Sure, go ahead. Just don't take too long. The show's starting in about twenty minutes."

"Hang on," I said, turning around to survey the crowd. "You gotta see this."

I saw my mother and the rest of our group sitting in the front row. The three seats closest to the aisle that belonged to me and my two housemates who'd headed off in search of funnel cakes were empty. Right behind the vacant seats sat Bubs and Chuckles in full costume. Moments later, Josie and Chef Claire strolled back to their seats carrying several funnel cakes on paper plates. Chef Claire noticed the two clowns immediately and chuckled as she shook her head. But Josie, already halfway through her first funnel cake, was oblivious to the clowns' presence. She handed out cakes and napkins to everyone then sat down and gave the deep-fried dough dusted with a generous portion of powdered sugar her undivided attention. She polished off the first cake, then immediately went to work on the second as she glanced around the circus ring with a big smile on her face.

Then Chuckles gently placed a gigantic clown foot on the seat next to her.

Josie stared at the foot then slowly turned around. She screamed, and her funnel cake went airborne as she scrambled out of her seat and made a beeline for the exit.

"Okay," I said, laughing. "My work is done."

I slipped through the curtains and made my way toward the back of the smaller tent where Wanda and her brother were stretching. I stood off to one side and watched as her brother bent at the waist and reached down with both hands. He placed his palms flat on the ground then lifted his legs into the air until his hands were completely supporting his weight. And if that weren't enough, he proceeded to do about a dozen pushups using just his hands. On the final pushup, he launched himself into the air and landed on his feet. He casually brushed the dirt and grass off his hands off then took a long drink from a bottle of water.

I shook my head as if to clear the cobwebs then watched Wanda slowly work her way into a split that ended with her legs fully splayed and flat on the ground. Then she used both hands to push herself up off the ground about a foot. Then she somehow rotated 360 degrees on one hand and transitioned into a backflip and landed on both feet. She caught the towel her brother tossed her and wiped her hands and face. Then she noticed me out of the corner of her eye and smiled.

"Hey, Suzy," Wanda said, tossing the towel back to her brother. "You slumming it tonight?"

"Hi, Wanda. Miguel. How on earth do you do stuff like that?"

"You start young, and you never stop," she said with a shrug.

"Constantly working to perfect your craft, right?"

"Is there any other way?" she said, gesturing with her hands to emphasize her point. "Thanks again for dinner last night. That was very nice of you."

"No problem. I was happy to do it," I said, glancing back and forth at them. Then I realized that Miguel had yet to speak a word in my presence. I let it go for the moment and focused on the reason I was here. "I'm sorry we didn't get much of a chance to chat last night. But you and Mr. Pontilly were in the middle of what looked like a pretty serious conversation."

"Yeah, we were," Wanda said, grabbing a bottle of water. Then she took a step back as Master Claude, in full costume, briskly walked past scowling at the ground without acknowledging any of us. "Try not to shoot yourself with the cattle prod tonight, Claude." He kept right on walking, but raised a hand and extended a finger without looking back. She watched him exit through the back of the tent where the animals were located and shook her head. "What a jerk."

"Yeah, I kinda noticed that," I said.

"I think you hurt his feelings last night when you didn't return the looks he was giving you," Wanda said, laughing.

"Oh, you saw that," I said, shrugging. "He's not my type."

"I'd be very disappointed in you if he was. Don't worry about it. I'm sure Grundella managed to take his mind off you," she said. "Did you stop by to wish us luck, or do you need something?"

Up until this point, I hadn't told anyone from the circus what Josie and I had seen the morning Samantha had gone overboard. But I had pretty much hit the wall as far as new information and clues were concerned. Since Grundella had mentioned over dinner that Samantha had been close to the two aerialists, I'd made the decision in bed last night to open up to them to see what they had to say. I was running the risk of word getting around about what I was doing and having everyone associated with the circus clam up. But Wanda and her brother seemed to be my best option for getting a better understanding of Samantha's state of mind as well as some idea about who might want to hurt her.

"I was wondering if I could ask you a few questions about Samantha," I said, then gave her a small smile.

"Samantha?" Wanda said, frowning as she glanced at her brother. "How do you know about Sammy? I'm sorry, but that doesn't make any sense. Were you a friend of hers?"

"No, I never met her," I said.

"Are you a cop?" she said, now studying me closely.

"No," I said with a casual shrug. "But sometimes I play one in real life."

128

Wanda stared at me, thoroughly confused, and motioned with both hands for me to continue.

"Talk," she whispered.

I did.

I spent a few minutes telling them the entire story, except for the part about our visit with Samantha's mother. When I finished, I slid my hands into my back pockets and rocked back and forth on my heels.

Compared to their warmup routine, it wasn't much of a workout, but I decided to count it.

"You saw somebody throw something off the boat?" Wanda said.

"Yeah," I said. "At first, I thought it was a bag of garbage. Then we found Queen B. in the middle of the River, and Samantha's body was discovered soon after. We sort of put two and two together."

"Garbage bag? She was probably wearing that dreadful plastic raincoat of hers," Wanda said to the brother with a sad chuckle. "I was always giving her a hard time about it." Then she again turned to Miguel. "I told you she didn't jump off the boat."

Miguel managed a small nod.

"Do you have any idea who might have wanted to hurt Samantha?" I said.

Wanda's eyes flickered as she thought about my question, and I got the distinct impression that she definitely had someone in mind.

"No one specific," she said eventually, then glanced around the tent avoiding eye contact. "Where's Queen B.?"

"A couple of people who work for me are taking care of her at the moment," I said. "What do you think we should do with her? She's a lovely little dog."

"She is," Wanda said. "Find her a good home would be my suggestion."

"So, there's no one from the circus she should go to?"

"No, absolutely not," she said. "This is no place for a cute dog like her. Queen B. should be spending her time sitting on someone's lap, and not in the middle of this nonsense."

"Did Samantha know that?"

"Yeah, she did. But lately, that dog was about the only thing that kept her grounded. I know Sammy hated to do it, but she said she was planning on giving the beagle to her mother."

"I see," I said, one of my suspicions confirmed. "Did Samantha talk about her mother? Or her childhood?"

"As much as she could," Wanda said. "Whatever memories she had about those days were buried pretty deep. And whenever they surfaced, I knew I was in for a long night." She turned to her brother. "Right, Miggy? Remember that night in Iowa when we found her out on the eighth-floor ledge?"

The brother nodded then stared down at the ground.

"Sammy had a lot of mental health problems," Wanda said. "Have you tracked her mother down yet?"

Seeing no reason why I shouldn't tell her, I nodded.

"We have."

"Maybe you could give Queen B. to her," Wanda said.

"I don't think that's a good idea," I said, shaking my head. "The mother is very unstable."

"How so?" Wanda said, cocking her head at me.

"She seems to slip in and out of lucidity. When she's out, she talks to her dead husband. Actually, she basically yells at him," I said, frowning at the memory. "And she does this really weird thing with her head."

"Something like this?" Wanda said, then did a spot-on impression of the mother's rotating head.

My mouth dropped open as I watched her.

"That's exactly it," I said, baffled. "How did you know that?"

"Sammy used to do it whenever she got really upset. It always freaked me out," Wanda said. "I had no idea it was something she learned from her mother." Wanda teared up and exhaled loudly then squeezed her brother's hand who continued to stare down at the ground. "Ah, Sammy. You poor thing."

I thought I heard Miguel choke back his emotions, and he slowly walked away.

"Miggy," Wanda called out. He stopped and looked at his sister. "Don't forget to eat before we go on." He nodded and resumed his walk. "Miggy was very close to Sammy," Wanda said as she watched her brother's departure.

"Can I ask you something?"

"Sure. Why stop now?" she said softly as she dried her eyes.

"Does your brother talk?"

"With difficulty, yes," Wanda said. "But he's not comfortable talking around strangers."

"Shy?"

"Not really. He lost a piece of his tongue that left him with a heavy lisp," Wanda said. "He's embarrassed by it."

"How do you lose a piece of your tongue?" I said, raising an eyebrow.

"Actually, he bit it off," Wanda said with a small shrug. "We were doing an outside show in Colorado a few years ago, and the wind was really tricky that day. He missed the net coming down at the end of our act and landed face first. He was lucky he didn't kill himself."

"Geez," I said, grimacing. "Yuk."

"That's a word for it," she said. "For Miggy, it was pretty much spoons and straws for several weeks. Actually, it was Sammy who took care of him while he recovered."

"Were Miguel and Samantha an item?" I said.

Wanda chuckled softly and glanced up at the ceiling of the tent briefly before looking back at me.

"Well, that's a tough one to explain," she said.

"Why's that?"

"Sammy had a really hard time with boundaries," Wanda said. "You know how most people use a hug and maybe a kiss on the cheek to express their friendship?"

"Sure," I said, listening closely.

"Well, Sammy had a bad habit of kicking things up a couple of notches when it came to showing affection."

"I'm not following."

"Think it through," Wanda said.

I did. Then the penny dropped.

"Oh, I see," I said, my face flushing with embarrassment. "Really?"

"Pretty much," Wanda said. "And after Miguel, how shall I say this, was the beneficiary of her affection, he fell hard for her. And he was crushed when she couldn't maintain that *affection* on a consistent basis."

"So, Samantha wasn't looking for a committed relationship?"

"Samantha? Committed? Institutionally, maybe. Relationship, not a chance," Wanda said, chuckling sadly as she shook her head. "You know how some people always seem to flit through life?"

"I do."

"Well, Sammy sort of lurched through hers," Wanda said with genuine affection. "When she wasn't running into walls, she was bouncing off them."

"I see. That's so sad."

"It was," she said. "My relationship with her was different from the one she had with the others."

"How so?"

"Even though I'm twenty years younger than she was, Sammy liked to say that I was the mother she never had," Wanda said, again tearing up. "And she was always doing things to test the boundaries. Then she'd expect me to pull her back and get her in line. It was not a role I either enjoyed or was very good at."

"So, I guess it's safe to say that she was what you might call a lost soul," I said, choosing my words carefully.

"Welcome to the circus," she said, then glanced up at the clock hanging on the wall. "Look, I need to get going. If you want to talk later, you know where to find me for the next few days."

"Thanks, Wanda. I appreciate it."

"Just promise you'll find a good home for Queen B."

"You have my word on that," I said, nodding. "Can I ask you one more thing?"

"Tenacious little thing, aren't you?" she said, laughing.

"Yeah, I really need to start working on that," I said, shrugging. "What were you and Mr. Pontilly discussing last night? It seemed really intense."

"It was," Wanda said. "We were talking about our contract. It's just about up, and Miguel and I have decided to leave the Pontilly *family*."

"And he's not happy about it?"

"No, he's not," she said.

"Why are you leaving?"

"This circus is dying," she said. "And Pontilly just can't accept that fact. And as soon as more countries wake up and ban those disgusting wild animal acts, pretty much all he'll have left is some jugglers and clowns. And Grundella's dog act until she drinks herself into the gutter."

"Unless he can convince you and your brother to stay?"

"I'm sure that's definitely part of his thinking," Wanda said. "But like I told him last night, he can always recruit another aerial act."

"But not one as good as yours, right?"

"Well, thank you for the compliment," she said, beaming at me. "No, I doubt if he can find another act as good as ours. Especially for what he's willing to pay."

"Maybe he'll offer you part ownership," I said.

"He already has," she said. "But like I told Pontilly last night, what's twenty percent of nothing worth?"

"Ouch," I said, laughing. "I take it he didn't respond well to that one."

"No, that made him pretty grumpy," she said, grinning. "He's still not speaking to me."

"Where are you guys going to go?"

"We're heading to Vegas. We've been offered a slot with one of the Cirque du Soleil shows," she said. "No more touring. At least for the foreseeable future."

"We're going to have my bachelorette party in Vegas soon," I said. "Maybe we'll get a chance to see you up there."

"I'd like that," she said, nodding. "When's your wedding?"

"August."

"Congratulations. Is your fiancé here with you?"

"No, he's away on a work trip."

"What does he do?"

"He's a disaster relief consultant."

"Interesting," she said, nodding. "We could use someone with his talents around here."

Chapter 17

I headed back to the main tent, gave the scowling Josie a grin and a finger wave as I walked past our seats, then continued up the aisle and found Chief Abrams near the entrance.

"Not willing to face the music yet?" he said, laughing as he nodded in Josie's direction.

"No, I thought I'd give her a few more minutes to cool off," I said, grinning. "Where did she go after the clowns got her?"

"I found her hyperventilating outside," he said. "When she calmed down, she grabbed a couple more funnel cakes and went back to her seat. You do know you're going to pay for this, right?"

"I do," I said. "But it was so worth it. I just had a chat with Wanda, the aerialist."

"What did she have to say for herself?"

"Quite a bit, actually," I said. "She doesn't buy the suicide story."

"You don't think she was involved?" Chief Abrams said, gesturing for me to follow him away from the entrance so we could speak without being overheard.

"No, I don't," I said. "Samantha considered Wanda her surrogate mother."

"What about the brother?"

"Samantha broke his heart," I said.

"Interesting. Always a good motive," he said. "They were in a relationship?"

"I don't think so," I said. "Apparently, Samantha wasn't shy about sharing her affections."

"I see," he said, nodding. "So, Samantha was *close* to several of the other performers?"

"According to Wanda," I said.

"She didn't happen to mention any possible suspects, did she?" he said, waving to a group of people who were making their way through the crowd.

"I floated the question, but she didn't bite," I said. "But I got the feeling she had definitely somebody in mind."

"Okay, that might be helpful. What's your take?"

"At the moment, I'm leaning toward jealousy. If Samantha was making the rounds with all the men who work here, one of them could have done it as payback for breaking their heart."

"Or maybe the girlfriend of one of her conquests," he said, glancing over at me.

"That's an interesting thought. But the woman would have to be pretty strong to throw her off the boat like that," I said, then an idea popped to the surface when I remembered Wanda's warmup routine. I frowned and stared off into the distance.

"What is it?" the Chief said. "You've got that look."

"No, it couldn't have been her," I whispered.

"I'm gonna need a bit more, Snoop."

"I was just thinking about strong women and landed on Wanda. I watched her warm up backstage earlier, and she's incredibly powerful," I said, still frowning. "No, it couldn't have been her."

"Is she close to her brother?" he said.

"She certainly seems to be. And protective."

"And she decided to take Samantha out because she broke her brother's heart?" the Chief said, giving it some serious thought. "Yeah, I can make that work. We've certainly seen stranger things."

"No, I don't like it," I said, shaking my head. Then I caught a glimpse of someone sitting by himself about halfway up one of the grandstands. "Well, what do you know?"

The Chief followed my eyes and spotted the man right away.

"What the heck is he doing here?" I said.

"Maybe he's a fan of the circus," the Chief said, not taking his eyes off him.

"Yeah, and I'm a spokesperson for Jenny Craig."

"It looks like he's by himself," the Chief said.

"Did you ever hear back from your contact about Bobbie's background?" I said, staring at Robert Tompkins, Bella Johnson's friend and caretaker.

"I did," he said. "He hasn't had so much as a parking ticket over the past twenty years."

"So, Bella's caretaker is an upstanding citizen who's simply devoted to her well-being," I said.

"It certainly looks that way," he said.

"Then what the heck is he doing here?" I said.

"Like I said, maybe he's just a fan," the Chief said.

"You really believe that, Chief?"

"I do not," he said, glancing over at me.

"I need to figure out a way to have a little chat with Bobbie," I said.

"Well, it's going to have to wait until intermission," the Chief said, as the lights dimmed. "Showtime."

I snuck another look at Bobbie as I walked down the aisle to my seat. I sat down just as a spotlight appeared in the center of the ring. Josie glared at me, and I gave her an evil grin.

"Having a good time?" I said, watching as Mr. Pontilly appeared through the curtains and stepped into the spotlight.

Josie fumed and ignored me as we focused on the ringmaster. He spread his arms wide and in a booming voice welcomed everyone to the *world-famous* Pontilly Family Circus. Tonight's performance started with a group of jugglers and people on unicycles, then transitioned into several people juggling while riding unicycles. Bubs and Chuckles were two of the performers and proved to be quite proficient in both skills.

"It must be hard riding one of those things with those gigantic shoes," I said, glancing over at Josie.

"Shut it."

"Yeah, those feet are enormous," I said, again watching the show play out a few feet in front of me. "They'd probably take up a whole seat."

The jugglers finished to a nice round of applause, and the next twenty minutes were filled by a combination fire breathing and sword swallowing act that made my stomach roil. Judging by the oohs and aahs of the people sitting behind us that transitioned into whispered gasps when one of the performers slid a gigantic sword down his throat, everyone else's reaction seemed to be pretty much the same as mine. The final act before intermission, as Mr. Pontilly made sure everyone in the crowd understood, was Master Claude and the elephant.

I thought about heading outside but decided to stay and see if Master Claude's public treatment of the elephant was any better than his behind the scene methods. The elephant, dressed in a ridiculous silver costume wrapped around its head and back, slowly made its way through the opening in the curtain and lumbered into the ring. Master Claude led the elephant through a series of walking tricks, then had the animal stand on its back legs and trumpet loudly.

"This is making me sick," Josie said, shaking her head.

"Yeah, just think how much pain he had to put the animal through to get her to do that," I said.

"I'm glad you shot him," Josie said.

"So, you've forgiven me?" I said, glancing over at her with a grin.

"Not a chance," she said, slugging me hard on the shoulder.

The punch, along with my outburst it generated, got us a stern look of rebuke from my mother.

"Knock it off," she whispered through clenched teeth.

"Sorry, Mom," I whispered, leaning toward her. "But she hit me."

"That's nothing like I'm going to do to you if you don't shut up," my mother said with another violent whisper.

For a moment, I was transported back to my childhood as I remembered how many times she had used the identical threat on me. I sat back in my seat, chagrined.

"This is all your fault," I whispered.

But Josie was staring wide-eyed out at the circus ring, and I followed her eyes. The elephant, who must have heard my outburst, was slowly walking directly toward me. Master Claude was doing his best to get the elephant's attention and refocused on the act, but the gigantic beast was ignoring him. The crowd emitted a nervous titter as the elephant walked toward the edge of the ring, and several people gasped and froze in their seats in fear. The elephant, obviously recognizing me, came to a stop directly in front of my seat and gently draped its trunk over my shoulder. I stroked it, and the crowd began to laugh and applaud.

Then the elephant began poking its trunk into the big bag of peanuts sitting on Josie's lap.

"Hey," Josie said to the elephant. "Get your own bag."

Soon, the entire bag had disappeared, and the elephant turned its head when Master Claude jerked the back of its ear with the bullhook. The elephant expelled a torrent of peanuts from its trunk that hit the trainer with surprising force right in the face. Master Claude grabbed his eye then hit the elephant hard with the long pole, and the audience immediately turned on him and began to boo.

Seconds later, the lights dimmed, and Mr. Pontilly raced into the ring under the spotlight and announced intermission. I remained in my seat and gave the elephant's trunk one final stroke. Then the animal turned and slowly walked back through the curtains without any assistance from the embarrassed and enraged Master Claude. Both men chatted angrily with each other as they followed the elephant then glanced over their shoulders and glared at me as the lights came up.

"Now there's something you don't see every day," Rooster said, laughing.

"Well played," Josie said, patting my hand.

"I can't take you anywhere," my mother said, shaking her head.

"What was I supposed to do, Mom?" I said, getting to my feet. "The elephant walked right up to me."

"Serves him right," Chef Claire said. "Did you see the way he treated that poor animal?"

"I did," my mother said. "And it's despicable." Then she wheeled on me. "But that doesn't excuse your behavior, young lady."

"Relax, Mom," I said. "No harm, no foul. And the crowd loved it. Did you see the way those peanuts came out of its trunk? It was like the elephant was using a machine gun. Remind me to bring a bag of hard candy tomorrow night."

"Oh, I'm not coming back tomorrow," Josie said, spotting the two clowns who were mingling with the crowd.

"Coward," I said, laughing.

"Are you kidding?" she said. "I almost peed my pants when I saw that clown's foot next to me."

"Yeah, I thought that was a nice touch on his part," I said.

"Enjoy it while you can," Josie said. "Your day is coming."

"Josie," my mother said, focusing her laser-stare on her. "Whatever you plan to do as payback, just make sure you don't pull any shenanigans at the wedding. Got it?"

"I wouldn't think of doing something like that, Mrs. C.," Josie said. "I'm thinking about saving it for their honeymoon."

"That would be fine," my mother said, grinning at me.

"C'mon, Doctor Doolittle," Josie said. "I'll buy you some ice cream."

"No, thanks," I said, glancing around the crowd. "I need to go have a chat with somebody, and the ice cream would probably melt by the time I got back."

"I'd never let that happen," Josie said, shaking her head.

144

"Yeah, I forgot who I was talking to for a moment," I said, finally spotting the man I was looking for standing in a long line. "But I think I will get one of those sausage and pepper sandwiches."

Chapter 18

I slid into the sandwich line directly behind Bobbie, aka Robert Tompkins, caretaker of the old woman with the rotating head. I got my first good look at him and decided he was somewhere in his early sixties. He was over six-feet tall and still had a full head of unkempt, salt and pepper hair. I tried to formulate my opening question, but the smell of Italian sausage and onions and peppers sizzling and snapping on an enormous grill captured and held my attention for several seconds.

"That smells incredible," I said, deciding it wasn't a bad opener and might provoke a response.

"It certainly does," Bobbie said, turning his head around. Then he flinched when he eventually recognized me. "You."

"Me?" I said, going for coy. "Do I know you?"

"I saw you and your cop friend driving out of Bella's place the other day," he said, giving me the once-over.

"Oh, that's right. Now I remember," I said, nodding. "You were driving the red truck."

"You really upset her," Bobbie said. "It took me the rest of the day to get her settled down."

"That certainly wasn't our intention," I said, taking a step forward as the line moved. "But since we were giving her the news about Samantha, it only makes sense that she'd be upset, right?"

"Yeah, I suppose it does," he said, exhaling loudly.

"By the way, I'm Suzy Chandler," I said, extending my hand.

"Bob. Bob Tompkins," he said, returning the handshake. "But you already knew that, didn't you?"

"Yeah, you caught me," I said, grinning at him. "How's she doing?"

"Bella's pretty much back to normal," he said.

I frowned, and he didn't miss the look on my face.

"Well, normal for her," he said.

"How long has Mrs. Johnson been like that?"

"A very long time."

"And you look after her to keep her from being institutionalized?"

"That's part of it," he said, taking another step closer to the promised land.

"There's more?" I said, cocking my head at him.

"That's really none of your business, is it?" he said, his eyes narrowing.

"No, I'm sure it's not," I said, shrugging. "I'm just curious about a few things."

"Like what?" he said as we approached the head of the line.

"Mrs. Johnson said that you hadn't been around for a few days."

I glanced at the grill and tried to decide which Italian sausage had my name on it.

"So?"

"So, nothing," I said, shrugging. "Like I said, I'm just curious."

"You ever hear the expression that curiosity killed the cat?" he said, also checking out what was on the grill.

"Sure," I said. "But I'm more of a dog person."

"Good for you," he said, then turned to the person taking orders. "One sausage and pepper sandwich, please."

"Make that two, please," I said, peering over his shoulder and pointing. "And could I have that sausage right there?"

"Does it really matter which one they give you?" he said, glancing over his shoulder.

"Attention to detail always matters. Especially when it comes to food," I said. "How long have you lived in Bucks Bridge?"

"Thirty-two years," he said, reaching into his pocket.

"No, these are on me," I said, glancing at the drink choices. "I think I'll have a beer. Can I get you one?"

"That sounds good," he said, putting his wallet away. "Thanks. Do you usually make it a point to buy food for strangers?"

"We're really not strangers anymore, Bob," I said, handing over a pair of twenties to our server. "Keep the change." I accepted my sandwich and beer and took a sip to minimize the spill factor once I started walking. "I noticed some picnic tables outside when I came in. You want to go sit down?"

"Lead the way," he said, taking a long sip from his cup of Labatts.

We sat down at an empty table across from each other and spent a few minutes in silence as we worked our way through our sandwiches. There's something about eating sausage and peppers outside in the fresh air that always puts a smile on my face. I wiped my mouth with a napkin then took another sip of beer as I watched a solitary speedboat cruise upriver on top of the calm water against the backdrop of a gorgeous sunset.

"Can I ask you a question?" I said.

"Well, since you bought me dinner, how can I say no?" he said, polishing off the last of his sandwich.

"You really enjoy the circus, don't you?" I said, taking a sip of beer and staring at him over the top of my cup.

"Not really," he said, shaking his head. Then he stared across the table at me. "What are you talking about?"

"Well, since this is at least the second time you've been to this show, I just assumed you were a big fan."

His eyes narrowed, and he was confused by my comment.

"Second time?"

"Yes, tonight, and last month in Brockville," I said, setting my beer down. "You were there, weren't you?"

"How the hell did you know that?"

"Lucky guess," I said with a shrug. "I could eat another one of those sandwiches."

"Me too," he said, still baffled by the fact I knew he'd been at the Brockville performance. "Did you see me over there at the show?"

"No," I whispered. Then I stared into his eyes. "But how else was Samantha going to get home if you didn't show up to give her a ride?"

"Who are you?" he said, his eyes wide.

"I'm Suzy," I said, gulping down the last of my beer.

"You and that cop think I might have been involved with what happened to Sammy, don't you?" he said, sliding his cup of beer to one side.

I thought about his question for several seconds as I glanced back out at the River. The memory of seeing Queen B. perched on the channel marker and the sight of Samantha stuffed inside the body bag flared, and a thought that had been nagging at me surfaced. I finally made eye contact and shook my head.

"Not unless you were on that boat," I said. "And the only way you could have been on the boat was if you worked for the circus."

"Maybe I was a stowaway," he said, reaching for his beer.

"Hiding out among the tigers, right?" I said, grinning.

"There you go," he said, smiling. "No, I wasn't on the boat. And I'm sure U.S. and Canadian Immigration have me and my truck on video crossing back and forth at Ogdensburg that night."

"Excellent point," I said, officially crossing him off my list of suspects. "Samantha had dropped a hint to her mother about a surprise."

"She did," Bobbie said. "But I had no idea what it was."

"She wouldn't tell you?"

"No, she was afraid I was going to blab to Bella and ruin the surprise," he said, draining the last of his beer and crushing the paper cup onto a ball. "I guess we'll never know now."

"It was a toy beagle," I said. "Actually, she's a Queens Beagle."

He stared at me in disbelief.

"Really?" he said, then waited for me to confirm it with a nod. "Wow. Sammy really was trying to see if they might be able to get back to what she called *happier times*."

"Happier? Everything I've heard is that her childhood was horrible," I said, frowning.

"Oh, it was miserable," he said. "Except for the dogs. It was the one thing Sammy and Bella could do together in relative peace and quiet."

"And she thought it was time to see if she and her mom could recreate a piece of her childhood," I said, out loud to myself as I again stared out at the River that was quickly slipping into darkness.

"Yeah," Bobbie whispered. "She wanted to at least give it a shot."

"Samantha rarely wrote letters to her mom," I said, again to myself. Then I looked across the table at him. "But she wrote to you often, didn't she?"

He stared back then slowly nodded.

"The letters started coming about five years ago," he said.

"And she wanted you to do what, broker some sort of peace between her and her mom?"

"Eventually," he said. "But Sammy kept putting off coming home until the time was right. Maybe getting the dog was part of it."

"But why would she write to you and not her mom?" I said.

"I was as close to bad memories as she was willing to get," Bobbie said, shrugging. "At least, that's what she said. I think I was some sort of lifeline for her."

"That's so sad," I whispered. "So, she told you she was working with the circus?"

"No, absolutely not," he said. "She never gave me an address or phone number."

"How did you figure it out?"

"Recently, her letters had been arriving more frequently," Bobbie said. "And I was able to pick up a bit of a pattern. You know, like she might be part of some group that was touring the country."

"Smart," I said, nodding.

"Thanks," he said. "So, I did some research on all the usual suspects. Rock bands, dance troupes, you name it. But I couldn't find anything. Then one day on a whim, I tried to put myself in her shoes. Where would I go if I wanted to get away and be around other people with similar backgrounds and not be asked a lot of questions? I hit on the idea of the circus, and sure enough, I found her with her dog act on the Pontilly website."

"You were going to surprise her in Brockville, weren't you?" I said, trying to manage the jumbled thoughts and questions bouncing around my head.

"I was," Bobbie said. "I was worried she was getting cold feet about visiting Bella."

"Why was that?"

"Her last letter mentioned coming home soon, then she said something that stuck with me."

"Like what?"

"I can't wait to see you and my mom. *If I make it*," Bobbie said.

"That's interesting," I said. "You were worried she was either in danger or maybe about to hurt herself?"

"I was," Bobbie said. "So, I decided to check out the opening night of the tour in Brockville to see if I could convince her to come home with me."

"And when you got to Brockville, you heard that she'd jumped off the boat and drowned."

"Yeah, that's the story I was told," he said, nodding.

"But you didn't buy it as a suicide, right?"

"I had my doubts. I could tell she was very excited about the prospect of reconnecting with her mom."

"Why didn't you tell Bella about what happened to Samantha after you found out she was dead?"

"I couldn't do it," he said, tearing up. "I was worried the news would send her to a place she wouldn't be able to get back from."

"So, you decided to wait and see if the cops figured out who she was and did it for you?"

"Yeah," he said. "I'm such a coward."

"I think you're being a bit hard on yourself," I said.

"Maybe," he said, exhaling loudly. "Do you think she killed herself?"

"No, not a chance," I said. "You came here tonight to see if you might be able to figure out who killed her, didn't you?"

"I did," he whispered. "But I really don't know where to start."

"Are you coming back tomorrow night?"

"I certainly am," he said. "And if necessary, my plan is to follow them on tour all summer."

"Oh, let's hope it doesn't come to that," I said, grinning at him. "I mean, how many sausage and pepper sandwiches can one person eat?"

"A lot," he said, laughing.

"I need to ask you another question," I said, feeling the nagging itch from a subject I thought had been put to bed.

"Go ahead."

"It's about Samantha's beagle."

"What about it?" he said, raising an eyebrow.

"I have her," I said, exhaling audibly. "And I've found a great home for her, but I feel compelled to ask if you think Mrs. Johnson should get the dog."

"No," Bobbie said with a sad, extended shake of his head. "That wouldn't be a good idea."

"Because Mrs. Johnson is slipping away, isn't she?"

"Yeah," he said, choking back his emotion. "I'm afraid she's fading fast. And she's getting to be too much even for me."

"I'm so sorry," I said. "And you wouldn't want the dog, right?"

"No, that's not possible."

"Because you're not a dog person?"

"No, that's not it. I love dogs."

"Then it's because the dog would bring back too many memories, right?"

"Yes. And most of them bad."

"Okay," I said, getting to my feet. "It looks like the show's about to get started. I need to run. Maybe I'll see you tomorrow night."

"Sure, I'll keep an eye out for you," he said, staring out into the darkness. "Thanks again for the sandwich and beer."

"Anytime," I said, patting his hand as I walked past him toward the tent.

"Hey, Suzy?" he said, calling after me.

"Yeah?"

"You're positive she didn't jump off that boat?"

"Yes. I am."

I walked back inside the tent and headed straight for the sausage and peppers stand. I ordered six sandwiches then carried them in a box back to my seat. The Chief was standing in front of our group, laughing and chatting with my mother. He refused my offer of one of the sandwiches, and I passed them out, keeping one for myself. My mother and Chef Claire both declined, but Rooster and Paulie quickly accepted and began working their way through them. I handed one to Josie, then we both glanced down at the two that remained in the box.

"I bought too many," I said.

"No, you didn't," Josie said, getting to work on her first one.

"Hey, Chief," I said, motioning for him to come closer. "Remind me to update you on a conversation I just had with Bobbie Tompkins."

"Yeah, I noticed you two were having a chat," the Chief said. "I can't wait to hear all about it. Find me after the show."

"Will do," I said, taking a big bite of my sandwich.

"Did he say why he's here tonight?" the Chief said.

"He did," I mumbled, then glanced down the row to make sure my mother hadn't seen me talking with my mouth full.

"And?"

"He's here for the same reason we are."

"I see," the Chief said, nodding. "I take it he's not a big fan of the circus."

"Nothing gets past you," I said, grinning at him as I held my sandwich out to him. "You sure you don't want a bite?"

"No," he said, shaking his head. "Actually, I've already had three."

"You little pig," I said, laughing.

"Says the woman who buys them by the box."

Chapter 19

The second half of the show began with Grundella and her dog act. The woman who had knocked back at least two bottles of wine while sitting next to me at dinner the previous night seemed to be a little fuzzy and was moving slow. She was wearing the same tails and top hat outfit that Samantha had been wearing in her website picture, but it was baggy and in desperate need of an alteration. Grundella gave the crowd a big wave as she forced a smile and introduced the dogs in a gravelly voice that sounded like she'd polished off a pack of Marlboro right before showtime.

"I think she's still hungover," I said to Josie.

"Yeah, she's definitely a step behind the dogs," she said, staring out at the ring. "Do they look like they've been abused?"

"No, they don't," I said. "But it does look like their spirits might have been broken."

"Yeah, that's how I see it," Josie said, shaking her head in mild disgust. "And they're the ones with the short lifespan. Go figure."

We watched the collection of poodles, retrievers, and German shepherds work their way through a series of tricks and activities I was sure our house dogs could master after a few weeks of training. But the dogs were fun to watch, and the crowd gave them a big round of applause when they finished. Grundella stood in the center of the ring at the end of the act and took a bow. Then she seemed to wobble on her feet before leading the dogs back through the curtains.

"You want that last sandwich?" Josie said, eyeing the box.

"Knock yourself out," I said.

"You know, if we split it, then round down, technically, we've only had two each," she said, glancing over at me.

"I like the way you think," I said, breaking the sandwich in half. I took a bite then focused on the ring as Mr. Pontilly stepped to the center to announce the next act that turned out to be a rehash of the juggling and balancing act we'd seen in the first half of the show.

"I think I'm having a déjà vu moment," Josie said. "Didn't we already see these guys?"

"We did," I said, then shrugged. "But everyone seemed to like them. Maybe Pontilly wanted to bring them back for an encore."

"Or he's running short on acts," Josie said. "Maybe he should consider eliminating intermission."

"And kill concession sales?" I said, shaking my head. "Not a chance."

"I wonder where Master Claude is with his tiger act," Josie said. "Not that I'm complaining."

"He's probably still pouting about what the elephant did to him," I said, laughing. "Now that's an act I wouldn't mind seeing again."

Pontilly again stepped to the center of the ring and drummed up another round of applause for the departing jugglers before announcing the next act. A new act, the old man said, someone certain to astound and delight, the latest addition to the Pontilly Family Circus who, according to Pontilly, was a distant cousin recently released from kidnappers who'd done everything in their power to force him to reveal how he performed his repertoire of astonishing illusions. But the man had withstood their torture and preserved the secrets that had been part of the Pontilly family for decades. I listened closely with a frown on my face.

"This guy missed his calling," Josie said, polishing off the last bite of her half sandwich.

"Used car salesman, right?"

"Oh, good one. I was thinking politician, but yours is better."

I focused on Pontilly as he made a sweeping gesture with his arm and introduced Iggy the Magnificent.

"A magician? You gotta be kidding me," I said, glancing at Josie.

"There's nothing like a little close-up magic in front of a thousand people, right?" she said, laughing.

We sat quietly as we watched the magician do his best to perform and entertain the audience. Even from the front row, I was having a hard time following along, and I was sure that the rest of the crowd were pretty much oblivious to what the magician was doing.

"Wanda said the circus was on its last legs," I said, shaking my head when the magician began doing a card trick. "I guess she wasn't joking."

"This guy would be great in a small club," Josie said, frowning. "But not here. Wake me up when he's done."

Mercifully, the magician's act didn't last long, cut short I was certain by the man's realization that he should probably get out of the ring before the crowd started to turn on him. Mr. Pontilly was obviously annoyed when he came out to introduce the next act, the grand finale that turned out to be Wanda and her brother's aerial act. The spotlights focused on them already perched high above the crowd. They were standing on opposite ends of the netting, and they both waved to the cheering crowd when the lights hit them.

For the next fifteen minutes, we were captivated by the two aerialists who performed individually on the trapeze, then finished with several somersaults and catches working as a pair. Wanda finished with a triple somersault, and her brother caught her with both hands. Then he released her, and Wanda dropped into the net, backflipped into the air and landed on the ground with both feet. Seconds later, her brother followed suit, and they trotted off waving to a standing ovation. They returned for an encore bow, then disappeared behind the curtains, and the lights in the tent went bright.

"Wow, they're really good," Josie said.

"Yeah, they're gonna fit right in with Cirque de Soleil," I said. "I can see why Pontilly is cranky about them leaving."

"That's gonna leave him pretty much high and dry," Josie said. "And if anything happens to his animal acts, he's not gonna have a lot left. Certainly, nothing I'd pay thirty bucks to see."

"You feel like stopping at C.'s on the way home for dessert?" I said, glancing at Josie and Chef Claire.

"No, I made a chocolate torte today," Chef Claire said. "And it's waiting at home as we speak."

"The one you're going to be serving at the rehearsal dinner?" Josie said.

"That's the one," Chef Claire said. "Your mom wants to make sure it pairs well with the dessert wines." Chef Claire gave us a small shrug. "And she wanted something to snack on while we're doing the binder session tonight."

"Crap. That's right. I forgot," I said with a scowl.

"Don't sound so excited, darling," my mother said.

"Sorry, Mom. I didn't know you were eavesdropping."

"Funny," she said.

"What's on the agenda tonight?" I said.

"Champagne, dinner reds, and dessert wines."

"Ooh. Not the briar patch. Are we doing a taste test?"

"Of course," my mother said, looking at me like I'd lost my mind.

"Well, why didn't you say so?" I said, leading the way toward the exit.

"I've been wondering something," Josie deadpanned to Chef Claire. "What champagne pairs well with sausage and pepper sandwiches?"

"One with bubbles," Chef Claire said, giving her a gentle shove. "Just walk."

Chapter 20

I grabbed a small glass of port from the line my mother had poured and motioned for Chief Abrams to follow me into the living room. Chloe tagged along and hopped up on my lap as soon as I'd settled on the couch. The Chief sat down across from me with a slice of chocolate torte on his lap and a glass of champagne in his hand. He raised his glass in toast then set it down and began working on his cake.

"So, what did Mr. Tompkins have to say for himself?"

"A lot, actually," I said, scratching Chloe's ears.

"Did he come across as someone who has nothing to hide?"

"He did," I said as Chloe spotted Captain entering the living room. She hopped off my lap and began playfully terrorizing the Newfie. Within seconds, they were rolling around on the floor. "And there was no way he was on the boat when Samantha and the dog went in the water."

"You're positive about that?"

"Yeah. He went to see the circus in Brockville," I said, taking full advantage of my dog-free lap to take a sip of port. "And he drove his truck."

"He told you that?"

"No, I brought it up, but he confirmed it."

"How the heck did you figure that out?" the Chief said, setting his fork down on his plate.

"It just seemed to make sense," I said, shrugging. "And when I saw him tonight, I figured he was at the circus for the same reason as us."

"Trying to find out who killed her," he said, giving it some serious thought. "Okay, I suppose I can buy that." Then he frowned. "Hey, wait a sec. There's no way he could have known she was dead before the Brockville performance. We didn't even know her name at that point."

"He was going to surprise her then drive her home to see her mom," I said.

"So, Samantha told him she was working in the circus?" the Chief said.

"No, he figured it out by himself. And it was pretty clever the way he did it."

"And when he didn't see the dog act during the show, he did some snooping around and discovered she was dead?"

"Yeah, I'm pretty sure that's what happened. We didn't go into the details. But he'd been in frequent contact with her over the years."

"That's interesting," he said, taking a bite of torte. He washed it down with a sip of champagne. "Samantha stayed in touch with him but not her mother. Did you get into how he became Bella's caretaker?"

"Not really," I said. "My guess is that he just sort of slipped into the role after her husband killed himself and Samantha disappeared."

"That's quite a sacrifice," the Chief said.

"Yeah, that's what I thought. He must have been a close friend of the family. Since he lived just up the road, I imagine he decided it was the neighborly thing to do. And Bucks Bridge is so small and remote he was probably Mrs. Johnson's only option. He did say that he was doing everything he could to keep her out of an institution."

"Based on what we saw the other day, I'm not sure he did her any favors," the Chief said with a shrug. "So, if we remove him from the list of suspects, then it definitely had to be someone from the circus who threw her off the boat."

"Nothing gets past you, Chief."

"Don't start," he said, stifling a yawn. "It's too late."

"Tompkins was worried about Samantha's safety," I said.

"Based on what she was telling him in her letters?"

"Yeah, she said something in her last letter that really got his attention," I said, pausing for effect. "I can't wait to see you and my mom. *If I make it.*"

"Okay," he said, nodding as he finished the last of his champagne. "So, she was concerned about her own safety. Has anybody mentioned if she was prone to paranoia?"

"No," I said, shaking my head. "Nobody's specifically mentioned it. But it's clear she was unstable. Her being paranoid wouldn't surprise either one of us."

"It certainly wouldn't," he said. "So, the big question remains. Why would anybody want to kill her?"

"I can't shake the idea that it had to be related to some sort of love triangle. At least, some weird variation of circus love," I said.

"Circus love?" the Chief said, laughing.

"I couldn't come up with a better term for it," I said, laughing along. "You know, brief, casual hookups among a transient population."

"Sure," the Chief said, grinning. "Circus love."

"And somebody got their wires crossed when they expected something more permanent," I said.

"Such as the aerialist, Miguel?"

"I don't know, Chief," I said, shaking my head. "He seems devastated."

"Maybe it's guilt posing as despair," the Chief said.

"Maybe," I whispered.

"I suppose we could just let it go," the Chief said. "They'll be gone soon."

"You know you don't mean that, Chief."

"No, I don't," he said. "Especially since she went overboard right in front of town. But I don't have a clue about how to shake the tree and get something to fall out we can use."

"I thought I might have a chat with Mr. Pontilly tomorrow," I said.

"What do you want to talk with him about?"

"Well, he definitely runs a tight ship, and he might have seen or heard something," I said.

"It might be worth a shot," the Chief said. "Maybe he gets chatty when annoyed."

"What makes you think I'm going to annoy him?"

"Let's call it a hunch," he said.

"Darling, I'm really going to need a decision from you," my mother said as she entered the living room carrying a bottle of champagne in each hand.

"Mom, I already told you that I like them both," I said.

"You need to pick one," she said, holding the bottles out.

"Fine," I said, then pointed to the bottle in her left hand. "That one."

"Really?" my mother said, frowning. "Are you sure you wouldn't prefer the Vintage Brut?"

"I'm sure," I said.

"Why?"

"Because it's three-hundred a bottle," I said, staring at her.

"You let me worry about that, darling," she said, then nodded. "The Krug it is. Don't go anywhere. You need to decide on the ports."

I watched her head back into the dining room and shook my head.

"Three-hundred a bottle?" the Chief said, staring at his champagne glass.

"Yeah, I know. She's insane."

"What's she giving you and Max for your wedding present? France?"

Chapter 21

Josie and I strolled through the acreage behind the Inn in the general direction of the welders who were making great progress constructing the various cages we needed for the rescue center. We waved to the group of high school kids we'd hired for the summer to help out and were pleased to see that the terraced picnic area behind the pond was beginning to take shape.

"I'm starting to see it," Josie said, coming to a stop to survey the overall scene.

"Yeah, it's going to look great," I said. "But I still think we're nuts."

"Oh, there's no doubt about it," she said. "But you know what your mom likes to say. Either go big or go home, right?"

"I guess," I said, staring at the cage area off to our left.

"Uh-oh," Josie said. "What is it? You've got that look."

"I was just wondering what sort of animals we'll be able to handle," I said, rocking back and forth on my heels.

"You mean, like an elephant and a couple of Siberian tigers?" she said, fixing a narrow-eyed stare on me.

"Now, there's an idea," I said, grinning back at her.

"Suzy, please," she said, shaking her head. "Don't even go there."

"Relax. I'm just wondering if we'd be able to handle something like that," I said. "I imagine the tigers could handle the winters. But I'm not sure about the elephant. How do they handle the cold?"

"I have no idea," she said. "But it doesn't matter because we aren't stealing the elephant. And we certainly aren't going to keep tigers onsite. Besides, we'd just be swapping one cage out for another. And that wouldn't do much for them."

"They'd be treated a lot better here," I snapped, turning defensive.

"They would. But that's not the point. They need to be taken to a reserve that's designed to take care of them," Josie said.

"So, you agree that they need to be removed from that circus?"

"Of course, I agree. But as despicable as it is, those animals still belong to Pontilly, and he's not doing anything illegal."

"Maybe," I said, staring off into the distance.

"Unbelievable. New topic."

"Sure. Knock yourself out," I said, glancing at her.

"Chef Claire and I booked our trip yesterday," she said.

"That was quick," I said, feeling a knot begin to form in the pit of my stomach.

"Yeah, we needed to jump on it before the cooking school filled up. We're starting with that right after we land. The classes

171

run for a week, and the school is at a gorgeous villa in Northern Italy. And we're going to be staying right onsite."

"It sounds amazing," I said, exhaling audibly.

"Yeah, it does. And after the first week, we're going to head to the Lombardy region. Chef Claire wants to spend some time researching the history of risotto and polenta."

"Why does she want to do that? I love her risotto and polenta."

"She says they're not authentic enough," Josie said, shrugging. "And while we're there, she wants to visit some cheesemakers. She says she needs to learn how to make her own Gorgonzola."

I laughed as we continued to walk toward the cage area.

"Then we're going to do some winery tours as we make our way south," Josie said, sounding more excited by the minute. "Chef Claire wants to head to Tuscany from there to study breadmaking. Then it's on to Naples."

"That's where pizza was invented, right?"

"It is," Josie said. "And Chef Claire has found some famous pizza chef who's willing to spend a few days working with her."

Josie noticed the look on my face and stopped walking. I also came to a stop and stared back at her.

"Are you okay?" she said.

"I'm just going to miss you guys, that's all," I said.

"I'm sure you and Max will be just fine. And we're only going to be gone for a month at a time."

"For now," I whispered.

"Suzy, I'm never leaving this place," Josie said. "You do know that, don't you?"

"Yeah, I guess I do," I said, nodding. "But we can't say the same thing about Chef Claire."

"No, we can't. Look, you need to remember that Chef Claire is different from us. She's like…an eagle."

"An eagle?" I said, frowning.

"Yes, she's built to soar," Josie said. "And explore."

"Now you're saying she's somehow confined? Maybe even trapped living here?"

"Don't pout," Josie snapped. "I'm not saying anything like that. But Chef Claire is in a different place than we are at the moment. When you boil it all down, we're basically a couple of nesters. But she's an explorer who needs to see a lot of places and have as many adventures as she can before she finally decides to slow down and maybe kick back a bit."

"I'm being selfish again, aren't I?"

"Yeah, but we forgive you," she said, gently punching me on the shoulder. "Just let her do her thing. In a few years, she'll either put permanent roots down here, or she'll decide to go big and probably end up being a major star with her own show and her name on a line of cookware."

"There's no reason she can't do that from here," I said.

"No, there probably isn't," Josie said. "But she's not convinced of that yet. So, just sit back and enjoy watching what she does. It's gonna be one heck of a ride."

"Okay," I said as I began walking. "I'll do my best. What's that thing you always say about choices?"

"The reason so many people have a hard time saying yes is that they know that as soon as they do, they'll be saying no to a whole bunch of other options."

"That's the one," I said. "I never actually paid close attention to what it really means."

"Geez, thanks," she deadpanned.

"You know what I mean. But now I get it."

"Because you've said yes to Max and motherhood, right?"

"Yeah."

"Any regrets?"

"Not a one," I said, grinning at her.

"I'm glad to hear that," Josie said. "Because your mother would have a stroke if you started having second thoughts now."

"Oh, that reminds me," I said. "She said last night that we only have one more thing to decide."

Josie stared off, deep in thought.

"I can't imagine what it could be," she said. "She's got the whole week planned out down to the minute."

"Think it through," I said, cocking my head at her.

"Okay," Josie said, then frowned. "Oh, no. Really?"

"Yeah. The wedding dress and bridesmaids' gowns."

"Let me guess, she's scheduled a fitting for all of us," Josie said.

"*Fittings*," I said. "Starting next Monday."

"We should have gone with your idea of just getting married out on the River," Josie said.

"Bathing suits and a keg is starting to sound pretty good, huh?"

"What are you gonna do? At least, it's keeping her young," Josie said.

"She doesn't need any help," I said. "So, you're really going to go to cooking school?"

"I am. I'm looking forward to it."

"Make sure you show the teacher how you slice garlic with your scalpel," I said, laughing.

"Yeah, Chef Claire said the same thing."

"All this talk about what you're going to be doing in Italy is making me hungry."

Josie came to a sudden stop and nodded at me.

"I could eat."

Chapter 22

After a lengthy fridge-raid, Josie and I headed back down to the Inn and spent half an hour saying hello to all the dogs that were outside in the play area enjoying the warm weather. Today's count, not including our four house dogs, was up to eighty-one, and I put my hands on my hips as I looked around at our collection of residents that came in all shapes, sizes, and breeds.

"Are you thinking what I'm thinking?" Josie said.

"That it's time we had a weekend adoption event?" I said.

"Yeah, we haven't had one in a couple of months," I said, nodding for her to follow me back inside. "What time are Sammy and Jill starting today?"

"I think they're working the afternoon shift," Josie said. "They said something about taking the boat out this morning."

"I have some good news for them," I said, holding the back door open for her.

We headed into the registration area and spent a few minutes chatting with a couple of friends who had brought their lab in for his annual checkup. Josie headed off with the dog, and a few minutes later, Sammy and Jill arrived with Tripod, their three-legged spaniel, leading the way. Queen B. was nestled in Jill's arms, and she set the dog down on top of the counter. The beagle cocked her head at me as I walked over to the counter and began scratching her ears.

"You don't miss a trick, do you?" I said, laughing at the quizzical look the dog was giving me.

"Do you have any news yet?" Jill said, her voice a combination of anticipation and nervous energy.

"Actually, I do," I said. "I've spoken with everyone who might have an interest in taking her."

"And?" Jill said, her voice going up about an octave.

"And I'm really sorry, Jill," I deadpanned, pausing for effect then grinning at her crestfallen expression. "But you and Sammy are just going to have to take her."

"You're so mean," she said, playfully swatting my hand. "Really?"

"Yeah, she's all yours."

"Oh, that's great," Jill said, hugging the beagle. "Thank you so much."

"No, thank you," I said. "And Josie and I were talking about doing a weekend adoption event. Could you and Sammy check the calendar and see if we might be able to pull one together before the end of the month?"

"I think we can make that work," Jill said, laughing as she accepted the beagle's licks and kisses.

"She's a happy girl," I said, then grabbed my car keys. "Look, I need to run out for a while. Our sales rep is supposed to drop by later this afternoon. I left the food and supply order on my desk."

"I'll make sure he gets it," she said. "Where are you going?"

"I thought I'd run off and join the circus," I said, waving over my shoulder as I headed out the front door.

I made the short drive and parked on the street in front of the temporary marquee. I headed down the path and walked into the main tent. It looked a lot different in the daytime than it did when lit at night, and I noticed several performers scattered around chatting and practicing their routines. Far above the ground, I watched Wanda and Miguel working on what appeared to be a new routine and again marveled at the speed and strength required to pull off what they were diligently trying to perfect.

On my way into the area behind the main tent, Iggy the Magnificent headed in my direction lugging two large suitcases. The magician was obviously mad, and he got even angrier when one of the heavy cases banged hard off one of his knees. He dropped both suitcases and began rubbing the knee with both hands as he cursed up a storm.

"That's gotta hurt," I said.

"Good call, Captain Obvious," he said, glaring at me.

"There's no need to get snarky," I said. "Running off to join normal society?"

"What?" he said, pausing to glance up from his work on the knee.

"Where are you going?"

"He fired me," the magician said. "After one performance. Can you believe that?"

I decided to keep my opinion about his question to myself.

"Family, huh?"

"What?" he said, confused.

"Nothing," I said. "I guess it's not the best venue for a magician, right?"

"No, it's not that," Iggy said as he continued to massage his knee. "The old man refused to pay me for last night's show. He said I ran short."

"And then he fired you?"

"No, he fired me right after I called him a bottom feeding parasite," Iggy said.

"Yeah, that would probably do the trick," I said, shrugging. "What are you going to do now?"

"Probably go back to where he found me," Iggy said.

"Where did he find you?"

"I was a street performer in Cornwall," he said, grabbing his suitcases.

"Cornwall?" I said, trying to recall the touring schedule. "That's right. The circus was up there just before they came here. Pontilly saw you perform and offered you a job?"

"Pretty much," he said. "But getting fired is the best thing that could have happened. The guy's a total control freak."

Not waiting for a response, he headed across the tent to the main entrance then disappeared from sight. I flinched when I heard a soft thump a few feet away. I turned around and saw Wanda grinning at me as she bounced a few times in the netting and came to a stop.

"Oops," she said, laughing. "Missed it again."

"Nice of you to drop in," I said. "What on earth is that new trick you're working on?"

"It's a triple with a little twist," she said. "It's hard to explain. What brings you by?"

"I need to have a little chat with Mr. Pontilly," I said.

She frowned but said nothing.

"What's the matter?" I said.

"Just try to go easy with him," she said, heading for the ladder that would take her back to the top of the platform. "He's in a really bad mood today."

"I'll do that," I said. "Say, when are you guys taking off for Vegas?"

"Very soon," she said, stopping to turn around. "Are you coming to tonight's show?"

"I wouldn't miss it."

"Then you'll be able to tell people you saw our final performance with the *world famous* Pontilly Family Circus," she said as she climbed the ladder two rungs at a time.

I headed through the curtains and glanced around the empty space. Then I heard loud voices coming from the wardrobe room. I hung back and listened, trying to decide if I should interrupt.

"You need to relax, Mr. Pontilly."

It took me a second, but I eventually put a name to the voice. Chuckles. Then the other clown, Bubs, chimed in.

"Yeah, Mr. Pontilly. You'll come up with something. You always do."

"You two are no help," Pontilly said. "And it's not like anybody is handing over thirty bucks to watch you."

"With all due respect, Mr. Pontilly," Chuckles said. "That's not very nice."

"Yeah, Chuckles and I work our butts off for you," Bubs said. "And when was the last time we didn't do everything we could to help you out?"

"I'm sorry to take it out on you two," Pontilly said. "But this thing is falling down around my ears. Maybe I should just get out now."

"You can't do that," Chuckles said with a touch of panic in his voice.

"Yeah, what would happen to all of us?" Bubs said. "We're family."

The old man let loose with a bitter cackle.

"It'll turn around," Chuckles said.

"With what?" Pontilly said, then began a hacking cough that lasted a long time. "Wanda and Miguel are out of here tomorrow."

"We still have time to help them change their mind," Bubs said in a guttural voice that made the hairs on the back of my neck stand up.

"No, that's not an option," Pontilly said.

"We should have been working on them earlier," Bubs said. "And been more persuasive."

"It's too bad Sammy went off the boat," Chuckles said. "She probably could have convinced Miguel to stick around."

"Don't remind me," Pontilly said. "By the way, have you seen Grundella today?"

"I think she's still sleeping it off," Chuckles said. "You need to get her under control, Mr. Pontilly. At this rate, she's not gonna last long."

"A third-rate dog act led by a drunk and an animal tamer who won't get out of bed," Pontilly said. "What a lineup."

Deciding I had eavesdropped long enough, I tapped on a metal pole outside the entrance to the wardrobe room and poked my head in. All three of them turned to look at me.

"Good afternoon," I chirped. "Sorry to pop in unannounced."

"Hello, Ms. Chandler," Pontilly said. "Come on in. These two were just leaving."

"How are you doing?" I said to both clowns as they left. They managed grunts and small waves as they passed. I sat down in the chair the old man was pointing at. "Good show last night."

"You really think so?" he said, frowning at me.

"Well, I loved the trapeze artists. And the elephant act certainly ended with a bang," I said, then couldn't resist taking a gentle jab. "The magician, not so much."

"Yeah, sorry about that," he said, shaking his head. "I should have known better. But I was desperate."

"You gotta fill a couple of hours, right?"

"Indeed," he said. "How can I help you?"

Okay, Suzy. Showtime.

"Well, I was wondering if you could help me," I said, starting slowly. "I thought I should check with you before you left town. I'm trying to find out if there's someone who might want to take Samantha's dog if she does happen to turn up."

"I seriously doubt if that's going to happen," he said.

"Yeah, probably not. But you never know. Dogs have an amazing way of surviving and showing up when you least expect it."

"Okay," he said, giving me a puzzled frown. "Why do you want my help? Based on what I've heard, isn't that your job?"

"Fair point," I said, nodding.

Score one for the old man.

"Oh, I'm sure we'd be able to find a good home for the dog, but I always like to make sure there isn't a family member or friend available before we do that."

It was far from my best effort, but I thought it was strong enough to hold up.

"Well, unless you've managed to locate her family, I don't think that's going to be an option," he said.

"Sure, sure."

"And as far as friends go, all of Sammy's are here with the circus. And unless one of them has already raised their hand offering to take the dog, I think we can also rule that out."

"What about friends from the old days?"

"Old days? I'm sorry, I'm not following you."

"You know, back when you first found her on the street," I said, tossing my line into the water.

"I see you've been talking to some of my people," he said, staring at me.

"Not really," I said, shrugging. "It's just that I heard you sometimes find people to work for you who are, shall we say, momentarily down on their luck."

"What about it?" he said, officially on the defensive.

"Well, I was just wondering if there was anybody she was close to in the old days who might want the dog as a reminder. You know, to take the dog as a tribute to Samantha's memory."

"I would imagine that the people she was hanging around with back then are all either dead or in prison," Pontilly said without emotion.

"So, she was actually living on the street when you found her?"

"Basically, yes," he said.

"How did you recruit her?" I said, going for casual. "I mean, it's not every day that somebody comes up to you on the street and asks if you want to join the circus."

"Claude is not without his charms," Pontilly said with a grin.

"You have him pimping for you?" I blurted, momentarily caught off guard by his comment.

"Strong word," he said, frowning. "I prefer the term recruiting."

"And after he brings people here, you work your magic to close the deal?"

"You make it sound unsavory," he said, leaning back in his chair. "But trust me, what I offer them is a way out. And while circus life can be hard, it's certainly a better option than what most of them have to look forward to."

"After they start working for you, you train them?"

"We do," Pontilly said. "With practice, most people can learn enough to be part of the show. You've seen our jugglers and unicyclists."

"I have," I said, nodding. "They're good."

"Thank you. To a person, they were all recruited the same way," he said, draping a leg over his knee. "Even the ones who can't develop performance skills are still valuable workers behind the scenes. There are countless tasks that need to be done to keep a circus running."

"Yeah, I get that," I said, then an idea floated to the surface. "You used Samantha to recruit as well, didn't you?"

"Yes," he whispered. "From time to time."

"Because she, like Claude, also had her charms?" I said, frowning as I cocked my head at him.

"She did. And they were quite formidable," he said. "But she hadn't done any recruiting in several years."

"Since she was past her prime?" I said, my temper coming to a slow boil.

"Yes," he said, casually. "I'm afraid our recruitment process is more suited to our younger staff members."

"I hope I don't offend you, Mr. Pontilly," I said. "But I think that's a despicable thing to do."

"I'm sorry you feel that way," he said. "It's just part of doing business."

"That's funny," I said.

"What's that?"

"Just the way some people justify their behavior by putting the *it's just business* label on it. That must come in handy."

"Your not liking it doesn't make it less true," he said, staring at me.

I decided it was time to shift gears before I gave in to the urge to punch the old man.

"Had Samantha been having a tough time lately?" I said. "I mean before she jumped off the boat."

"That's a tough question," he said. "It was always hard to tell with her."

"Take a wild guess."

"I'm starting to find your tone most annoying, Ms. Chandler."

"Yeah, I really need to start working on that."

The old man chuckled then fixed his stare on me.

"If I were to hazard a guess, I'd have to say that, yes, Sammy had been having a tough time of late."

"Because?"

"Because it's what she did," he said with a small shrug. "One day, she'd be worrying about her dogs. The next, her coffee wasn't hot enough. Other days, she'd be worried about being stalked."

"What about love problems?"

"What about them?"

"Did she have them?"

"Don't we all?" he said with a blank stare.

"Fair point," I said, remembering how much I was missing Max and making a mental note to call him later. "So, Samantha wasn't happy."

"I think that's a logical assumption," he said with a frown.

"Why's that?"

"Because she committed suicide by jumping off the boat," Pontilly said.

"Oh, yeah," I said, then shrugged.

Given the rather circular nature of our conversation, I decided to put my cards on the table. I sat quietly as I formulated my approach.

"You seem troubled, Ms. Chandler," he said, breaking the long silence.

"I am," I said, nodding.

"And why is that?"

"It's because I don't think Samantha jumped off that boat," I said, studying his face to gauge his reaction.

But apart from a slight narrowing of his eyes, he didn't give anything away. In fact, he didn't even seem surprised to hear me say it. Maybe he'd been thinking the same thing.

"Why do you say that?" he whispered.

"Because if she loved Queen B. as much as everyone says she did, she never would have jumped off the boat with the dog."

"Interesting," he said, nodding. "And you think that someone from the circus threw her overboard?"

"It's a little hard to think anything else, Mr. Pontilly," I said.

"Yes, I suppose it is," he said, glancing around the wardrobe room. "But why would anybody want to do that? Sammy was troubled, but at the same time, she was no trouble. If that makes any sense."

"Yeah, I think I get it," I said, floundering as I tried to decide if the old man was lying to me. "She never said anything to you that made you worry?"

"Apart from her occasionally talking about leaving the circus, not a thing," he said.

"Samantha was thinking about leaving?"

"She would mention it from time to time," he said. "She talked about trying to reconnect with what was left of her family. Her mother, I believe. When Sammy first brought it up, I told her it was probably better if she didn't reopen that old wound. But she was quite determined to give it a try. Personally, I've always believed that old wounds should be left alone. Or to put it in your parlance, let sleeping dogs lie."

"Probably good advice," I said. "Okay, I think I've taken up enough your time, Mr. Pontilly. And you've got a show tonight. I imagine you've got a lot to do."

"Will you be coming to the performance?" he said, getting up from his chair and extending his hand.

"I wouldn't miss it," I said, accepting the handshake. "And it might be the last chance I get to see Wanda and Miguel."

"Yes, I suppose you're right," he snapped.

"Sorry I mentioned it," I said. "Old wound, right?"

"No. Actually, that one is still bleeding."

"Yeah, I imagine it is. I noticed Claude didn't make it back last night after the elephant shot him with the peanuts. Will he be performing tonight?"

"If he knows what's good for him, I'm sure he will," the old man with a casual shrug.

I left the wardrobe room and glanced around. Everyone appeared to still be practicing in the main tent, so I made a left and headed for the area where the animals were being kept. I slowly made my way past the two cages where the tigers were stretched out and yawning.

"Yeah, I'd be bored too," I said, coming to a stop. "You poor guys."

One of the tigers perked up and slowly approached. It pressed its head against the bars of the cage then let loose with a guttural growl that definitely got my attention. I stared back at the cat then continued on my way. About a hundred feet further back, I saw Claude standing in front of the elephant who was again chained to the post anchored into the ground. The elephant recognized me and flipped its trunk in the air and emitted what sounded like a happy squeak.

"That's the best you can do?" I said, laughing.

Then the elephant trumpeted loudly, and I flinched from the noise. Claude turned around, and I couldn't miss the eye patch he was wearing.

"The peanut did that?" I said, staring at the patch.

"I think I've got a detached retina," Claude said, obviously still annoyed.

"Good shot," I whispered to the elephant.

"What?"

"Nothing," I said. "You look like a pirate."

"Do you need something or did you just come back here to mock?"

"Actually, I came to see the elephant," I said, gently stroking the elephant's trunk. "How are you today, Beulah?"

The elephant draped its trunk over my shoulder and left it there.

"Man, that's heavy," I said. "She could do some real damage with that if she wanted."

"Tell me something I don't know," Claude said, turning on a hose and squirting water on the animal's back.

"She likes that," I said, nodding at the hose.

"It's about the only thing she likes these days," he said.

"Well, you can't really blame her, right? Chained to a post all day."

"What do you want?"

"I was wondering if I could ask you a couple questions about Samantha," I said, giggling as the elephant began toying with one of my ears.

"What about her?"

"I'm just curious about what she was like," I said. "And you obviously knew her pretty well. Since you were the one who recruited her."

Claude turned the hose off and tossed it on the ground.

"You been talking to Pontilly?"

"I have. He said you're one of his main recruiters. At least when it comes to finding new women to work here."

"So?"

"So, nothing. I was just wondering what Samantha was like."

"She was nuts," Claude said. "At least most of the time."

"Did you know that when you recruited her?"

"Yeah, sort of. But Sammy was different back then," Claude said, grabbing a brush and scrubbing the elephant's leg with it. "She was always odd, but she got worse over time."

"How so?"

"Sammy had a hard time focusing on the important stuff," Claude said.

"Circus stuff?"

"Yeah, pretty much," he said as he continued scrubbing the elephant with the brush. "And over the past few months, she couldn't stop babbling. She was like a rabid parrot. Yak, yak, yak. She was driving all of us nuts."

"Were the two of you close?" I said, going for casual.

Claude laughed as he tossed the brush into a bucket and hosed down the elephant's leg.

"Yeah, we had our moments. You want details?"

"No, that's quite all right, thanks," I said, grimacing. "Are you performing tonight?"

"I am," he said. "Fortunately, I only need one good eye." Then he glared at the elephant and sprayed the hose in her eyes. "No, thanks to you."

"Don't do that," I snapped.

"Do what?"

"Spray water in her eyes. She obviously doesn't like it."

"I really don't give a crap what she likes," Claude said. "Or for that matter, what you like."

"Okay, fair enough," I said, glancing around the immediate vicinity. I spotted the cattle prod on the ground. "I guess it's really none of my business."

"There you go," he said, laughing. "Finally, something we can agree on."

"What's that on her back?" I said, nodding at the elephant.

"What? Where is it? I don't see anything," he said, taking a couple of steps closer to the enormous creature.

I grabbed the cattle prod and slowly crept forward then jabbed it into his back. Apparently, the water from the hose he'd gotten all over himself kicked up the voltage a couple of notches, and Claude jerked violently before collapsing on the ground. For several seconds, I was convinced I'd killed him. But he gradually came to, then groaned and closed his eyes again. The elephant cocked her head at the man lying at her feet then stuck her trunk into the water trough and filled it. Then she turned her head and expelled a stream of water into Claude's face. When I was certain he would eventually recover, I patted the elephant's trunk then quickly made my way out the back and took the long way to where I was parked. I hopped in, still stunned by my behavior, and headed for home driving way too fast.

I glanced at myself in the rear-view mirror and shook my head.

"Are you out of your mind?" I said to myself.

I continued to sneak the occasional look at my crazed expression in the mirror, then remembered where I'd just come from.

"Maybe it's contagious."

Chapter 23

I parked in the driveway and headed up the driveway to the house. I entered the kitchen and spent a few minutes greeting all four house dogs before stretching out on a couch in the living room. I drifted off to sleep with Chloe tucked under my arm and dreamt hard of circus acts and caged animals. I, too, was locked in a cage, and I peered through the bars and saw Master Claude pointing accusingly at me as two clowns and Mr. Pontilly threw peanuts at my face and laughed at my plight. When I realized I was in the cage with a couple of tigers who hadn't eaten in a week, I screamed in my sleep and woke myself up.

I fed the dogs, let them out to stretch their legs and take care of business then took a long, hot shower. I pulled on a pair of sweats and draped a fresh towel over my shoulders. On a whim, I grabbed my laptop and sat down on the couch. I had no idea what I was looking for, but Claude's comments about Samantha's inability to focus on what he considered important circus business or keep her mouth shut had stuck with me and begun to nag.

I went to the Pontilly website and studied the photos of the various performers, many of their faces now familiar. I reread the circus's history and the fake family bios. I had to give Pontilly credit. Over the years, he had developed the ability to create a persona for himself and his business that was timeless and grounded in circus tradition. And the action shots and short video clips on the website presented the circus as a magical place that people of all ages would enjoy.

I was just about to call it quits and grab a bit more shuteye when a lightbulb popped in my head. I rubbed my forehead as I waited for a useful search term to make itself known. I tapped my keyboard, hit the enter key and waited. I scrolled down the page then clicked one of the links and scanned the website's photos and videos, then moved onto the next.

On my fourth attempt, I hit the motherlode.

The website, like the previous three, was devoted to calling out examples of inhumane treatment of animals by various circuses. There were dozens of photos, but a handful of them caught my attention. One of them showed Claude holding the bullhook behind the elephant's ear with a Pontilly Family Circus sign clearly visible in the background. The next few photos were shots of blood and damage done to the ear by the hook. I felt my anger begin to build as I continued to work my way through the site. Then I discovered a video clip that showed Claude using the cattle prod on the elephant. The video then cut to Claude using a whip on the two tigers.

I was pretty sure the video had been shot on a cellphone, and I forced myself to keep watching even after my blood boiled and my stomach churned. When I almost threw up on the couch,

I forced myself to stop. I placed my laptop down on the coffee table in front of me and dried my eyes with the towel.

"Oh, Samantha," I said, exhaling loudly. "I'm so sorry."

I heard a knock on the kitchen door, then it opened, and a voice called out.

"In here, Chief," I said, tucking my legs underneath me on the couch.

"Hey," the Chief said, then noticed my red eyes. Obviously concerned, he sat down next to me and studied me closely. "What's the matter?"

I pointed at the laptop that was still open to the page I'd been reviewing. He leaned forward and spent a few minutes scrolling through the photos. Then he watched the video with a scowl. He pushed the laptop away and shook his head.

"That's disgusting."

"And illegal, right?" I said, glancing over at him.

"I'm sure it is."

"I want Claude arrested," I said. "And the old man as well. They can't be allowed to keep getting away with this crap."

"You're right," the Chief said.

"I think Samantha must have been the one who sent the photos and video to that website," I said. "And when Claude found out, he was worried she was about to get his acts banned and ruin his livelihood. So, he decided to throw her off the boat. He said this afternoon that Samantha was having a hard time remembering what was important and keeping her mouth shut."

"This afternoon?" the Chief said.

"Yeah, I stopped by earlier today to have that chat with Pontilly," I said as I started to towel my damp hair. "Then I had to do an intervention with Master Claude."

"Okay," he said, giving me an odd look. "Should I ask why?"

"You know me, Chief," I said with a shrug. "It's what I do. I wanted to see if I could get a bit more information about Samantha's recent moods. Maybe get a better idea if she was having problems with some of the people she worked with."

"I see," he whispered, sitting upright on the couch.

"You know, after tonight's performance, we can confront Claude about the photos and that video to see what he has to say for himself. If we put the squeeze on him, I think he might fold from the pressure."

"I'm afraid that's not going to be possible," he said.

"Why not? You could call in some backup from the state police. Don't worry, Chief, I'll be fine."

"There's not going to be a performance tonight," the Chief said. "It's been canceled."

"Canceled?" I said, scowling. "I know they ran a little short last night, but that's no reason to call it off."

"It's been canceled because he's dead," the Chief said, staring directly into my eyes.

In an instant, I felt my current and future life collapsing around me. My inability to mind my own business and control my base instincts had finally caught up with me. I stared at the wall as dozens of questions and concerns about my own wellbeing set my neurons on fire.

How the heck was I going to explain my actions to a judge and jury?

And Max?

Geez, how could I do something that stupid and ruin everything we had planned for the future before we even had a chance to get started?

And how on earth was I going to explain it to my mother?

My stomach did backflips as I imagined what those conversations would be like.

"I should have been more careful," I said eventually, still staring at the wall.

"What?" the Chief said, confused.

"I should have remembered the effect that water has on an electrical current," I said, finally making eye contact with him. "But I don't get it. I was sure he was okay before I left."

"I think I'm going to need a bit more, Suzy," the Chief said.

"No offense, Chief," I said. "But I don't think I should be having this conversation without my lawyer present."

"What on earth are you talking about?" the Chief said, exasperated.

"I'm talking about Claude. What else would I be talking about?"

"What about him?"

"I'm the one who killed him," I whispered.

"That would be a neat trick," the Chief said, shaking his head.

"What? Why do you say that?"

"Because Claude's not dead."

"He's not?" I said, stunned.

"Why would you think Claude's dead?" he said, doing a half-turn on the couch to get a closer look at me.

"Uh, I guess it doesn't matter. Never mind," I stammered, again looking away.

"Suzy," the Chief said in his best fatherly tone.

"Okay, I shot Claude with a cattle prod today," I said, shrugging. "He was terrorizing the elephant with a hose, and I lost it for a few minutes."

"Hence, your comment about the effect of water combined with electricity?"

"Yeah, I got him pretty good," I said. "And when you said somebody was dead, I just assumed you were talking about Claude." I forced a quick smile at him. "Whew. What a relief, huh?"

"Do you know how lucky you are that you *didn't* kill him?" the Chief said, glaring at me.

"Probably not as lucky as Claude," I said, going for lighthearted and missing by a mile.

"You're unbelievable."

"Yeah, definitely not one of my better moments," I said, then stared at him. "So, who's dead?"

"The old man," the Chief said.

"Mr. Pontilly's dead?"

"He is."

"Do you know how he died?"

"No. I got a call about an hour ago, then headed down there and called Freddie. He's at the circus right now doing his thing. And I need to get back."

"So, why did you stop by here?" I said, frowning.

"Actually, I was looking for your mother to see how she wants to handle getting the word out about tonight's show being canceled."

"I think she and Paulie were talking about going to Montreal to do some shopping. She's not answering her phone?"

"No, straight to voicemail," he said.

"She's been working pretty closely with Jackson on this one," I said. "We can swing by the store on our way. He'll probably know who to talk to."

"We?"

"Hey, it's just starting to get interesting. You can't cut me out now, Chief."

"Watch me," he said, laughing. "Besides, I don't think it would be a good idea for you to be around Claude. I imagine he's not very happy with you at the moment."

"I'll be fine," I said. "And stuck to you like glue the whole time."

"So, now you want my help."

"Hey, to protect and serve, Chief," I said, gently punching his shoulder. "Protect and serve."

Chapter 24

We walked past several stunned circus workers who were chatting quietly in various locations around the main tent. The performers were already in costume, and I spotted Bubs and Chuckles smoking cigarettes and toeing the dirt with their enormous clown feet. I followed the Chief through the curtains, and we found Freddie in the wardrobe room standing over Mr. Pontilly's body and talking with Detective Williams from the state police. The detective and I had crossed swords several times in the past, mostly over what he considered my inability to stop sticking my nose where it didn't belong. Over time, we'd been able to make peace and remain on relatively good terms, but when he spotted me, he frowned and looked at Chief Abrams.

"What's she doing here?" Detective Williams said to the Chief.

"Nice to see you too, Detective," I said, making a face at him. "I thought you'd want to talk to me."

"Why would I want to do that?" he said, frowning.

"I was probably one of the last people to see him alive," I said, casually tossing it out. "But if you don't want to ask me any questions, that's fine."

"You saw him today?"

"Nothing gets past you."

"Don't start," the Chief said, then glanced at Freddie who was kneeling down and examining the body. "What do you think?"

"Well, I don't see any wounds or bruises on him," Freddie said, carefully rebuttoning Pontilly's shirt. "My first guess is a heart attack. The guy had to be close to ninety."

"He seemed fine when I left today," I said, even though no one had asked for my input. "Maybe a little stressed."

"Stressed about what?" Detective Williams said.

"His circus was falling apart," I said. "He'd just lost his most popular act, and I think the wild animal acts are on their last legs."

"No, they're not," Claude said, entering the wardrobe room already dressed for the performance. The red suit with long tails looked ridiculous, but I had to concede that the black eye patch definitely added a touch of mystery to his outfit. He glared at me and pointed a finger as he glanced back and forth at Detective Williams and the Chief. "I want to press assault charges against this woman."

"Go right ahead, Claude," I snapped. "And I'll be filing animal cruelty charges right back at you. As well as showing every media outlet I can think of some interesting photos and videos of you torturing those innocent creatures."

Master Claude flinched, shut his mouth, but continued to glare at me. I held my ground and returned his angry stare with one of my own.

"Okay, let's take a step back," Detective Williams said, turning to Claude. "You say she assaulted you?"

"Yeah, she stuck me an electric cattle prod," he said. "And I have a feeling she also did the same thing when we were doing a show in Brockville."

The Chief stared at me, but I looked away and rocked back and forth on my heels.

"Suzy?" the Chief said. "What's he talking about?"

"I have no idea," I said to the wall. "He's obviously deranged."

"You want deranged? I'll show you deranged," Claude said, lunging for me.

The Chief inserted himself between us and shoved Claude back a few steps.

"You see what I mean?" I said, nodding at Claude. "Now, imagine that anger turned loose on defenseless animals."

"Did she do that to your eye?" Detective Williams said, staring at the eye patch.

"No," Claude said. "An elephant shot me with a peanut."

"Okay," Detective Williams said, confused. He glanced around before settling on me. "You stuck him with a cattle prod?"

"Maybe."

"Why on earth would you do that?"

"He was squirting water in the elephant's eye," I said. "Not to mention using the cattle prod on the poor thing. And a bullhook behind her ears. He also keeps the elephant chained up at least twenty hours a day."

"What should I be doing with it?" Claude said, bewildered. "Taking it for walks?"

"*You* shouldn't be doing anything with it," I said. "You shouldn't be allowed within a hundred yards of any animal."

I stared down at the ground and mumbled my way through an impressive string of whispered expletives.

"What did you call me?" Master Claude said, again taking a step toward me.

"You heard me," I said.

"Uh, if you folks wouldn't mind toning it down a bit," Freddie said. "I've got a dead body here I'm trying to deal with."

"Sorry, Freddie," I whispered, then snuck another glare at Claude.

"You still want to press charges?" Detective Williams said to him.

"Go right ahead, *Master* Claude," I snapped. "I'd love the chance to have this conversation in front of a jury."

Claude looked off into the distance for several seconds, then turned to Detective Williams.

"I'm going to need to give it some more thought," Claude said.

"I knew it. You're a frigging coward," I said, taunting him. "You're such a big man, Claude. Torturing defenseless creatures who can't fight back. You're nothing but a bottom feeding scumbucket."

Then Master Claude managed to work his way around Chief Abrams and decked me with a punch that caught me flush on the jaw. I fell backward and landed hard. In my dazed state, I heard what sounded like the crack of wood hitting bone that was followed by loud grunts and groans. I heard muffled voices and tried to clear my head. Flat on my back, I blinked several times up at the ceiling and waited for the cobwebs to clear. Through blurred vision, I watched Chief Abrams slide his nightstick back into its holder, then he helped me sit up. I gently rubbed my jaw, and when my eyes focused, I spotted Claude handcuffed to Detective Williams' wrist. With his free hand, he was rubbing a large knot on his forehead. His anger was gone, apparently replaced by fear and confusion.

"You need to dial it down, Chief," the detective said.

"Hold him steady so I can hit him again," the Chief said, his voice low and threatening.

"Dial it down," Detective Williams whispered.

"Did you hit Samantha like that before you tossed her off the boat?" I said.

"What?" Claude said.

"You know exactly what I'm talking about, Claude," I said, staggering as I climbed to my feet and felt the onset of a massive headache. "Did you come up with the idea all by yourself, or was it something you and Pontilly concocted as the best way to shut her up?"

"What are you talking about?" Claude said, giving me a wide-eyed stare. "I'd never hurt Sammy."

"Save it for your lawyer, Claude," I said, but was surprised by his reaction to my accusation. All of a sudden, I was less than certain about his involvement in her murder. But I still couldn't get past my utter contempt for the man wearing the ridiculous suit of tails. "Scumbag."

"All right," Detective Williams said, officially out of patience. "I have more pressing matters to deal with at the moment. What do you two want to do?"

I massaged my jaw as I stared at Claude and waited for his response.

"Well," Claude said, starting slowly and continuing to rub the knot on his head. "Given everything that's gone on today, and out of respect for Mr. Pontilly, I suppose I can let it go if she can."

"Let it go? You punched me in the face," I snapped.

"And you shot me with a cattle prod," Claude said, returning fire. "Twice."

"Prove it," I said, then tasted blood. "Not to mention everything you're doing to those poor animals."

"Lady, I'm just trying to do my job."

"Job," I said with a snort. "You call that a job?"

"Chief," Detective Williams said, shaking his head. "The next time you're thinking about letting her tag along at a crime scene, do both of us a favor and don't."

"Yeah, I really need to start working on that," the Chief said, staring at me.

"Funny," I said, scowling at him. "Good one, Chief."

"What do you want to do, Suzy? We've got a long night ahead of us."

"I suppose I can let it go," I said. "For now."

"Suzy," the Chief said, now glaring at me.

"Okay, fine. You can cut him loose. I won't be pressing charges."

"Finally," Detective Williams said, removing the handcuffs. "A glimmer of common sense looms on the horizon."

"Don't try to wax poetic, Detective," I said, still fuming. "It's not your style."

Master Claude rubbed his wrist, then took a final look at Mr. Pontilly who was stretched out on the ground with a fixed look of surprise on his face.

"I'll need you to stick around, Claude," Detective Williams. "We'll be questioning everyone at some point tonight."

Claude nodded, shot me a final dirty look, then left the wardrobe room. I continued to massage my jaw as I glanced down at Freddie who was still examining the body.

"I can't believe he punched you," the Chief said. "He's lucky I didn't get a chance to really work on him with my nightstick."

"It's about what I'd expect from someone like him," I said. "But I have to say, it was a good punch."

"I wish you would have pressed charges," the Chief said.

"It's not too late," Detective Williams said, studying me.

"I pushed him pretty hard," I said.

"Still, he was way out of bounds," Detective Williams said. "That's a line you don't cross."

"Yeah, I know," I said, deep in thought. "I was sure I could goad him into confessing that he threw her off the boat. But after I saw his reaction, I'm not so sure he did it."

"He did seem surprised when you confronted him with it," Chief Abrams said.

"Yeah, he certainly did," Detective Williams said.

"Maybe you could do a little digging around when you interview all of them later," I said. "Someone might let something slip."

"You're convinced she was thrown off the boat?" the detective said.

"I am. But if it wasn't Master Claude, who the heck was it?"

"Oh, this is interesting," Freddie said, glancing up at us.

"What have you got?" Detective Williams said.

"Take a look," Freddie said, lifting one of the old man's shoulders off the ground and turning the head to one side. He pointed at a spot behind Pontilly's ear. "I might be mistaken, but I doubt it."

"It looks like a needlestick," the Chief said, kneeling down for a closer look.

"That's definitely what it is," the detective said, shining a pen flashlight on the tiny wound. "I guess that changes our approach to the interviews, Chief."

"Yeah, it sure does. And we should probably get started," he said. "Where do you want to do them?"

"If they decide to start breaking down the tents, it's going to be too loud to do them in here. Let's herd everyone outside to where they've got all the picnic tables set up. I'll have my guys ring the area to keep an eye on things just in case anybody decides to try and slip away."

"Yeah, that'll work," the Chief said. "Have you got that list of employees?"

"I do," he said, handing the list over. "If you can start getting everybody outside, I'll get my guys organized."

"You got it," the Chief said, then looked over at me. "And since this is now officially a murder scene, you need to get out of here. Why don't you head on home and get some ice on that jaw?"

I gave him a quick salute that turned into a wave. Both cops left the wardrobe room, and I was left alone with Freddie.

"You sure you're okay?" he said. "That was quite a shot you took."

"I'll be fine," I said, nodding at the body. "What do you think they shot him up with?"

"It could have been anything," Freddie said with a shrug. "A hit of poison. Maybe some sort of amphetamine that caused his heart to race and eventually give out. Or a massive dose of a depressant."

"Like the stuff that's in sleeping pills?"

"Sure, it's possible."

"Or elephant tranquilizer?" I said, raising an eyebrow at him.

Chapter 25

Deciding not to press my luck, I followed Chief Abram's instructions and left the main tent. The Chief and Detective Williams, surrounded by a half-dozen state policemen, had already begun their interviews, and despite the considerable amount of pain I was in, I had to laugh when I stopped to watch the bizarre scene of various circus performers sitting across from the cops answering questions in full costume. I spent a few minutes admiring the gorgeous sunset then drove home slowly, occasionally checking the bruise on the side of my face in the rear-view mirror. I headed up the driveway just as Josie was leaving the Inn through the back door.

"Hey," Josie called out.

"You're just finishing for the day?"

"Yeah, Marjorie Wilson's spaniel decided it was a good idea to play chasey with a porcupine," she said, shaking her head. "I spent the last hour and a half pulling quills out of him."

"The poor guy," I said, frowning. "Is he going to be okay?"

"Yeah, he'll be fine," she said. "But I'm definitely ready for a glass of wine. It's been a long day."

"No argument from me," I said.

"You're back from the circus already?"

"No," I said, opening the kitchen door. "The show was canceled tonight."

"Canceled?" she said with a frown as we entered the brightly lit kitchen. "What on earth happened to your face?"

"Master Claude went full Tyson on me," I said, cocking my head to give her a better look.

"What?" she said, enraged. "He punched you?"

"Yeah, and it was a good shot," I said, rubbing my jaw.

"I hope he's rotting in jail at the moment," she said, gently reaching out to examine the bruise. "Geez, he got you good. You didn't lose any teeth, did you?"

"No, just most of my dignity," I said, grinning. "But I'm not pressing charges."

"Are you nuts? Why not?"

"I figure I'm still ahead," I said, pouring two glasses of wine and handing her one. "Two jolts from a cattle prod versus one punch."

"Two?" Josie said, taking a sip then heading for the living room.

I followed her and sat down on the couch. I took a sip then set my glass down.

"Where are the dogs?" I said, glancing around.

"Chef Claire stopped by the Inn earlier and said she was taking them for a walk," Josie said.

"She's a brave woman," I said.

"You said two times," Josie said. "What am I missing?"

"I had another encounter with him this afternoon," I said. "He started squirting a hose in the elephant's eyes. So, I nailed him with the cattle prod again."

"Then he punched you?" Josie said.

"No, he hit me when we were in the wardrobe room while Freddie was examining Pontilly's body."

Josie stared at me in disbelief then shook her head.

"You really need to work on your storytelling abilities," she said. "Let's back up several steps."

I spent a few minutes telling her the story then focused on my wine while she digested what I'd told her.

"So, somebody murdered Pontilly, but you don't think Master Race Claude had anything to do with it?"

"No, I don't," I said. "Pontilly was Claude's lifeline. Without him, the circus is probably going to go under, and there goes Claude's job. And for his sake, I hope he's eligible for unemployment because I'm going to make it my personal mission that no circus goes within a hundred miles of him."

"There's my girl," Josie said, laughing. "And you're not sure that Claude had anything to do with Samantha and Queen B. going off the boat?"

"Not anymore," I said, frowning. "I was sure he'd done it. But when I confronted him, it was impossible to miss his reaction. He seemed genuinely surprised, even offended, that I could accuse him of doing that."

"Even though he probably thought Samantha had sent the incriminating photos and video to that website?" Josie said.

"I guess," I said, frowning as I refilled our wine glasses. "And if they did think it was her, I'm sure he and Pontilly were furious with her. But maybe they thought they could ride out any bad publicity and convince her to keep her mouth shut."

"But why would Samantha spend all those years working for the circus and then decide to do something like that? She must have been aware that Claude was abusing those animals for a long time."

"Yeah, I don't get that either," I said. "Maybe she had a rare moment of clarity."

"Yeah, that must have been it," she said, laughing. "Well, I guess we'll never know why she did it. Or who threw her off the boat."

"It doesn't look like it," I said, rubbing my jaw.

"And I know how much you hate it when that happens," she said, then raised her glass in salute. "But you gave it your best shot. To a noble effort."

"A noble effort," I said, raising my glass.

The kitchen door opened and all four dogs came racing into the living room. We set our wine glasses down out of reach of the furiously wagging tails and spent a long time welcoming them home.

"Did they behave themselves?" Josie said to Chef Claire.

"They were great," she said, then tossed a plastic bag of dog jerky on the table. "But that certainly helped. As soon as I threatened to withhold snacks, they settled right down. What on earth happened to your face?"

"I got punched," I said.

"Who hit you?" she said, staring at my face.

"Master Claude," I said.

"The guy from the circus?"

"That's the one," I said.

"Where's my bat?" Chef Claire said, glancing around the room.

"It's okay," I said. "We came to an understanding. And he's already walking around with a lump on his head."

"He won't be walking around when I get through with him," she said. "Why did he punch you?"

"It was payback for me using the cattle prod on him."

"How did he know you were the one who shot him in Brockville?"

"He sort of put two and two together after I shot him this afternoon," I said, shrugging.

"Do you have any idea what she's talking about?" Chef Claire said to Josie.

"Yeah, I'll fill you in later," Josie said.

"Okay," Chef Claire said, stretching out on the couch then glancing at me. "Are you sure you don't want me to pay him a little visit?"

"No, but thanks."

Then Chloe noticed the bruise on my jaw and hopped up on the couch to inspect it. Then she placed a paw on my leg and gently licked the side of my face.

"Look at that," Josie said, shaking her head. "How do they know?"

"It is pretty amazing," I said. Then I flinched and stared off into the distance. "Duh," I eventually whispered.

"What is it?" Josie said. Then she nodded, and a smile appeared. "Of course. Why didn't we think of that earlier?"

"Are you two going to keep speaking in code, or would you mind explaining what the heck you're talking about?" Chef Claire said, making room for her two Goldens on the couch.

"Queen B.," I said.

"I'm sorry, but I'm going to need a bit more," Chef Claire said.

"The beagle knows who threw them off the boat," Josie said.

"And she might react if she saw whoever it was again," I said.

"You're going to take the dog to the circus?" Chef Claire said.

"Yeah, I think I might just do that," I said. "I can swing by with the dog in the morning. They'll probably be packing up, and I can use the excuse that I stopped by to give everyone a chance to say goodbye to the dog."

"That'll work," Josie said. "What time do you want to go?"

"You want to come with me?"

"Yeah, I wouldn't mind having a little chat with Master Claude," Josie said.

"Oh, count me in," Chef Claire said, then frowned. "No, that's not going to work. I need to be at the restaurant early to meet the vegetable guy." She glanced back and forth at us. "But feel free to borrow my bat."

"If we're starting early, then I'm going to bed to get my rest," Josie said, finishing her wine and getting to her feet.

"I need to call Max before I turn in," I said, reaching into my pocket for my phone but coming up empty. "What did I do with it?"

"Your phone?" Josie said.

"Yeah, I can't find it," I said. "I had it with me earlier in the car. And I know I had it with me when I was at the circus." I sat in silence trying to remember the last time I'd seen it. "I bet it fell out of my pocket when I landed on the ground after he punched me." Then I shrugged. "I guess there's no time like the present, huh?"

"You want to go now?" Josie said.

"Why not?"

"It's getting pretty late," Josie said.

"Oh, I'm sure they're still talking to the cops," I said, getting up off the couch.

"Okay," Josie said. "Let me call Jill to see if we can borrow the beagle."

Chapter 26

A sleepy and somewhat confused Jill greeted us at the door with the beagle tucked under her arm. Then she motioned for us to follow her into the kitchen, and we sat down. Sammy entered rubbing his eyes and shuffling his feet. Half-asleep, he mumbled hellos then sat down and immediately made room for Tripod on his lap. The three-legged spaniel hopped up with no assistance and glanced back and forth at me and Josie, his tail wagging double-time.

"What on earth happened to your face?" Jill said when she finally got a good look at me.

"I got punched. Long story."

"Who hit you?" Sammy said, suddenly wide-awake.

"The animal tamer from the circus," I said, waving it off. "But don't worry about that at the moment."

"Oh, I'm gonna worry about it," he said. "Where is he?"

"No, really, it's okay, Sammy," I said.

"Nobody gets away with that," he said, rubbing the spaniel's head. "Jill said something about you wanting to borrow Queen B."

"If that's okay with you guys," I said. "We think she might be able to identify the person who threw her and Samantha off the boat."

"Okay," Sammy said, frowning. "She's not going to be in any danger, is she?"

"No, she won't," I said. "And don't worry, we'll keep a close eye on her."

"I have to say that it makes me nervous, Suzy," Jill said, hugging the beagle. "Maybe we should tag along?"

"There's no need for that," I said. "The place is crawling with cops at the moment. Queen B. will be just fine."

"I don't know what I'd do if anything ever happened to her," Jill said.

"Sure, we get that. She'll be fine. You have our word." I glanced at Josie. "Right?"

"Absolutely," Josie said.

"You guys head back to bed," I said. "If we run late, we'll just take her back to our place tonight."

"No, we'll be up," Jill said. "Won't we, Sammy?"

"Do I get a vote on that?" Sammy said, glancing around the table.

"No," Jill said, laughing.

We laughed, then Josie tucked the beagle under one arm, and I followed her to the door. On the way to the car, Josie laughed again.

"They're like parents with a newborn," she said, rubbing the beagle's head.

"Like we'd ever let anything happen to her," I said, reaching out to scratch one of the dog's ears. "But it's nice to know you've found your forever home, right, Queen B.?"

The dog licked my hand as I opened the passenger door, and Josie climbed in. We made the short drive and parked in front. I hopped out and stood on the sidewalk surveying the scene.

"Where the heck is everybody?" I said.

"It looks like the place is completely shut down," she said.

"They must all be back inside the tent."

"Maybe the cops figured out who did it and made an arrest," Josie said, sliding the beagle into her other arm.

"I guess it's possible," I said. "But I don't hear anything. I thought they'd be taking everything down by now."

"Pontilly's dead," Josie said. "Maybe nobody knows what's going to happen next or what they should be doing."

"Whatever happened to *the show must go on*?" I said, heading for the main tent.

"Didn't the magician tell you that Pontilly was a total control freak?" she said, following me.

"Yeah, he did. If Pontilly never trained a successor, that could be a real problem. Maybe there's nobody here who knows how the whole operation runs."

"So, when in doubt, do nothing?" Josie said.

We stepped inside the main tent, dimly lit by a handful of nighttime security lights attached to a couple of the support poles. I looked around but saw or heard nothing.

"Weird," I said, heading in the direction of the wardrobe room to look for my phone.

"Spooky," Josie said. "And if you set me up with those clowns again, you and I are gonna have a serious problem."

"Relax," I said, laughing. "I'm sure they're out of costume by now."

Halfway across the ring, I spotted Grundella coming through the curtains that cordoned off the performer area from the main tent. She saw us, cocked her head, but continued heading in our direction doing her best not to stagger.

"What are you guys doing here?" she said, then spotted the beagle. "Hey, Queen B."

The beagle emitted a soft, guttural growl and tucked herself tighter against Josie's arm. I glanced at Josie who continued to watch the woman closely.

"That dog never liked me," Grundella said, shaking her head. "I guess she never forgave me for the time I had an argument with Sammy."

"What sort of argument?" I said, going for casual.

"I don't even remember what it was about. We'd been drinking all night," she said with a shrug. "But it was a big one."

I put Grundella on the list as a *doubtful maybe* then glanced around the tent again.

"Where the heck is everybody?" I said.

"Packing. The boat is leaving in half an hour," Grundella said.

"What? Where is the boat going?"

"Hopefully, somewhere in the direction of the nearest airport," she said. "The guys who've been driving the boat are figuring that out at the moment."

"Hang on," I said, shaking my head. "Back up a bit. Did the cops say you could all leave?"

"They did," Grundella said. "Right after they arrested Claude."

"They arrested him for killing Pontilly?"

"As soon as they found the syringe in his work bag," Grundella said, removing a flask from her pocket. "Boy, you should have seen the look on Claude's face. He was shocked when they found it. I guess he thought he had it hidden somewhere where nobody would ever find it."

"He thought nobody would ever find it his *work bag*?" Josie said, frowning.

"What can I say?" Grundella said with a shrug. "If Claude was any dumber, he'd need to be watered twice a week. What a piece of work he is."

"From what I saw at dinner, you couldn't wait to spend some more time with him," I said with a grin.

"Yeah," she said, frowning. "But not to discuss philosophy."

"Got it," I said. "So, where are you going to go?"

"Either rehab," Grundella said. "Or Germany to get an early start on Octoberfest. I can't decide."

"Octoberfest?" Josie said. "It's June."

"Hence, the early start," Grundella said.

"You're taking your dogs to Germany?" I said.

"Oh, the dogs," Grundella said, scowling. "I completely forgot about the dogs."

I glanced at Josie who was giving Grundella her death stare.

"Don't worry about the dogs," Josie said. "We'll take them."

"You will?" she said. "All nine of them?"

"All nine of them," Josie said. "You better get going."

"Good call. I don't want to miss the boat."

"Yeah, the boat. That's what I was talking about," Josie growled as she continued to glare at Grundella.

Grundella was about to take a sip from her flask then got a good look at Josie's face. Message received, she waved and quickly walked away.

"What a despicable human being," Josie said, staring after her.

"Concur," I said, scratching one of the beagle's ears. "But I don't think she was the one who threw Samantha and this little girl overboard."

"Me either," Josie said. "I think Queen B. dislikes her just as a matter of principle."

"Come on," I said, laughing. "Let's go find my phone. I'm starting to think that this was a dumb idea. Nine more dogs," I said, shaking my head.

"Yeah, I know," Josie said. "But they should get snapped up pretty quick. They all do some cool tricks."

"Hey, what about the circus?" I said.

"What about it?"

"If the boat is leaving in half an hour, that must mean they're just going to leave everything here."

"I guess it must," Josie said. "Your mom and the rest of the council isn't going to be happy about a bunch of circus crap getting left behind."

"No, she isn't," I said, then another thought bubbled to the surface. "We need to take the elephant and the tigers."

"What?"

"We can't leave them here," I said.

"Slow down a sec there, Daktari."

"What else can we do? And the work crew has finished enough of the cage work at the rescue center. We'll make it work."

"But just on a temporary basis, right?" she said, monitoring my reaction closely. "And as soon as we find someone who can take them, off they go. Right?"

"Sure, sure."

"Suzy, I'm not joking. We're not going to just swap one cage for another."

"Of course not," I said, heading inside the wardrobe room. I glanced around and spotted my phone half-covered in the dirt. "There it is."

I picked it up, wiped it off and was about to call Chief Abrams for an update when Bubs and Chuckles entered the wardrobe room wearing jeans and tee shirts.

"No, I think we should just head to California. Maybe work construction for a while until something better turns up," Chuckles said, then came to a stop when he saw us standing there.

Before I had a chance to say hello, Queen B. whelped and scrambled out of Josie's arms then hit the ground running.

"What the heck?" Josie said, racing out of the wardrobe room to chase down the beagle.

"Weird dog," Bubs said.

"She's been through a lot lately," I said, then gave them a wide-eyed stare when the lightbulb popped. "You. It was you."

"What are you talking about?" Chuckles said. Then a lightbulb of his own flickered, and he gave me a dark stare before turning to Bubs. "I told you she was snooping around for some reason."

"Yeah, you were right," Bubs said, scowling at me. "Well, I guess it's better she figured it out before we left."

"Yeah, we'll just take care of her then get on the boat," Chuckles said. "How do you want to do it?"

"Well, since she lives around here, we gotta assume she can swim," Bubs said.

"Unless we attach something nice and heavy to one of her legs," Chuckles said as calmly as if he were ordering a sandwich.

"That'll work," Bubs said, glancing around the wardrobe room.

While they were trying to decide what to use to send me to a watery grave, I followed Queen B.'s advice and made a beeline for the exit barely escaping Chuckles' lunge as I brushed past them. I took a quick look around and decided to head for the main tent. I was about to cut across the middle of the circus ring for the exit when I spotted Chuckles racing along the far wall to head me off. I knew I couldn't win the footrace, so I paused at the edge of the ring desperately scanning the area for an escape route. I turned around and took a step toward the performer area but saw Bubs standing in front of the curtains with an evil grin on his face I so wanted to knock off.

"Problem?" Bubs said, laughing.

"Maybe," I said, glancing back at Chuckles who was slowly walking toward me.

I took another look around then spotted the ladder that led up to the platform the aerialists had used during their performance. I stepped onto the bottom rung of the ladder then began my ascent while trying to clear my head about the possibility of falling sixty feet and missing the net. Halfway up the ladder, I glanced over my shoulder and saw both clowns staring up at me with bemused expressions.

"Where do you think you're going?" Chuckles said, laughing.

"Up," I said as I continued my climb.

"Should we go get her?" Bubs said to his clown mate.

"No, let's give her a minute," Chuckles said. "This is too much fun to watch."

"Her friend is going to be coming back soon," Bubs said.

"Don't worry about it. We'll deal with her when she gets here," Chuckles said. "What's she gonna do? Sic the dog on us?"

I reached the top of the ladder and stepped onto the platform. As far as platforms go, it wasn't much to write home about. It was secure but small, no more than a three-foot square piece of thick plywood painted black. I knelt down and grabbed the top rung of the ladder for support and glanced around then looked down.

"Wow," I whispered, my arms and legs trembling. "Probably not my best work."

"Hey, lady," Chuckles called out.

"Yeah."

"Now that you've seen the sights, are you ready to climb back down?" Chuckles said.

"No, I think I'll stay up here for a while."

"That's your plan?"

"Well, I really wouldn't call it a plan," I said. "It's barely a strategy."

"So, what's your next move?" Bubs said, unable to contain his laughter.

"You mean, before or after I pee my pants?" I said, peering down into the dim light.

"Just come on down," Chuckles said. "We just want to have a little chat with you."

"Yeah, and I'm Tinkerbell," I said. "No, I'm fine right here for the moment."

Then I remembered my phone. I fumbled for it, almost dropped it, then placed the call. He answered on the first ring.

"Suzy," the Chief said. "I was just about to give you a call. You'll never guess what happened."

"You found a syringe in Claude's work bag then arrested him for Pontilly's murder."

"How the heck did you know that?" he said, stunned.

"Lucky guess," I said, glancing around in all directions.

"Suzy," he said, going fatherly on me.

"I'll tell you later, Chief," I said. "Right now, I need a favor."

"Oh, crap," Chuckles said, staring up at me. "She's on the phone."

"Okay," Bubs said. "Let's go get her."

"I need you here, Chief," I said.

"Where are you?"

"At the circus. I need you now."

I hung up and glanced down at the two clowns who were slowly working their way up the ladder. Then I spotted a figure in the shadows climbing the ladder on the other side of the netting. I squinted into the darkness but was unable to identify who it was. Then I glanced down and thought about attempting a jump from the platform. But I was close to the edge of the net and wasn't sure I could hit it. And if I missed the net, I'd be giving a whole new meaning to the term, *stuck the landing.*

"Suzy," a man said through a heavy lisp from the other platform.

"Miguel?" I said with a frown. Then I glanced down and noticed that the two clowns were halfway up the ladder.

"Grab the trapeze that's right next to you," Miguel said.

"And hit them with it when they get to the top, right?"

"No, grab the trapeze and swing out," he said. "I'll catch you."

"Yeah," I said with a snort. "Like that's gonna happen."

"I'm serious," he said, grabbing the trapeze on his side and swinging out to the middle. Then he pulled himself up and hooked his knees over the trapeze and hung upside down. "Just swing out and let go when you get to me. I'll catch you."

"Are you out of your freaking mind?"

I squinted at him as his trapeze stopped swaying and eventually came to a stop.

"Can't you just swing over like Tarzan and grab me like they do in the movies?"

"If my trapeze went that far I would," he said with some effort. His sister hadn't been lying about the lisp. "Just swing out. Even if I miss you, you'll drop right into the net."

"You'll have to excuse me if I don't share your confidence," I said, taking another look down at the two clowns who were closing fast.

"You want to stay there and wait for those two to get their hands on you?"

"It's a little late in the evening for rhetorical, Miguel."

Then I glanced down again and saw another man climbing the ladder the clowns were on.

"That was fast," I said, staring down at the figure cloaked in shadows who was doing his best to climb while holding something in his hand. "Well done, Chief."

"You need to jump, Suzy," Miguel snapped. "Now."

"Hold your horses," I said, glancing back and forth at the two clowns and the guy hanging upside down about forty feet away. "I guess there's not a third option."

I snuck another peek over the edge of the ladder and realized two things; the clowns had almost reached the top, and the man climbing the ladder behind them wasn't the Chief. I frowned as I tried to process what was happening then felt a hand on my foot. I screamed and kicked at Chuckles' hand. But he continued to reach for my leg. I waited until one of his attempts failed to connect then stomped on his hand. The clown screamed in pain and let loose with a well-practiced string of expletives that rolled off his tongue. But he pulled his hand back. Unfortunately, Bubs was able to use both hands to grab my foot, and he held on tight.

I struggled to get my foot loose, then my running shoe came off in his hands, and Bubs fell backward momentarily, almost plummeting off the ladder. But Chuckles grabbed his shirt and pulled him back to safety. When both their heads appeared over the top of the ladder with huge grins, I kicked Chuckles in the face with my bare foot. I winced and began hopping around in pain. On my third bounce, I almost hopped right off the small piece of plywood. Officially out of options, I took a deep breath then grabbed the trapeze with both hands and jumped.

I closed my eyes and let loose with a primal scream as I soared through the darkness. Then I slammed into Miguel hard and caught the metal trapeze bar he had his legs draped over with my forehead. I immediately began sliding down Miguel's legs then his chest. For a brief second that seemed like a lifetime, I dropped like a rock but came to a sudden stop when a hand grabbed my left wrist. Seconds later, he grabbed my right arm, and I opened my eyes as I gently swayed back and forth suspended fifty feet above the ground.

"Next time, trying doing it with your eyes open," Miguel said through a loud groan.

"Don't nitpick," I snapped, still terrorized. Then I softened. "Good catch."

"Yeah, thanks," he said, grimacing in pain.

I glanced over my shoulder to see what the two clowns were up to and watched as the man who'd climbed up behind them reached out with what looked a stick and jabbed Bubs in the back. In the darkness, I thought I saw a small spark just before Bubs began to twitch and spasm.

Then the clown fell off the ladder and dropped like a rock. He hit the edge of the net that partially broke his fall, but he still landed with a loud thump on the ground.

"Oh, that had to hurt," I whispered as I stared down at the unmoving clown who'd landed face first.

"Trust me," Miguel said. "It does."

I looked back at the top of the ladder, and soon a spasming Chuckles fell from the sky and missed the net completely. But his fall was also partially broken when he bounced off the side of the ladder, and one of his legs went through a gap in the rungs. His body jerked and tried to change direction then I heard a crack I assumed was his leg protesting the sudden turn. Chuckles immediately confirmed my suspicion with a loud scream that filled the tent. His descent continued, and he landed hard on top of his partner in crime. Both men remained face down in the dirt unconscious.

I still wasn't sure who the other man on the ladder was, but I definitely needed to thank him. But that would have to wait. My arms were on fire, and I forced myself to look down. In the dim light, I saw Josie standing next to the net holding Queen B. in her arms. She was staring up at me shaking her head in disbelief.

"Whatcha doin?" she called out.

"Shut it," I said, then glanced up at Miguel. "Are you sure I'll hit the net?"

"You have my word," he said, adjusting his grip.

Then in the dim light, I saw the needle tracks on both his arms. My neurons surged as I closed my eyes tight and he let go. I fell for what seemed like a week screaming the entire way. I landed with a soft *plop*, bounced a few times then came to rest. I slowly opened my eyes and shrugged.

"That wasn't so bad," I said out loud to myself.

"Okay, Ms. Wallenda," Josie said, laughing. "Let's get you out of there."

I made my way to the edge on my hands and knees, then tried to imitate the backward roll I'd seen Wanda and Miguel use during their performance to exit the net. But my foot got stuck, and I ended up hanging upside down with my hair brushing the dirt as the net gently bounced up and down.

"Smooth," Josie said, unable to stop laughing.

"Yeah, definitely not my best work," I said, finally getting my foot loose then landing hard on the ground.

"What on earth happened to your forehead?" she said.

"I hit the trapeze bar," I said, gently pressing my fingers against the bruise that was already starting to throb. "Am I bleeding?"

"It doesn't look like it," she said, examining the wound. "But it's definitely dented."

"Funny," I said, climbing to my feet. "You found her."

"She was saying hello to the elephant," Josie said, rubbing the beagle's head. "I think they're buddies."

"I'm so glad she's okay," I said, brushing myself off. "Jill would have killed us."

I flinched when I heard Miguel land in the net behind me. Seconds later, he was standing next to us.

"Thanks, Miguel. I think you might have saved my life."

"Don't mention it," he said, glancing at the two unconscious clowns sprawled out on the ground. "Who the heck hit them with the cattle prod?"

"I have no idea," I said, staring at the back of the man who was climbing down the ladder.

"I need to go help Wanda with the packing," Miguel said, extending his hand. "Maybe we'll see you in Vegas sometime."

"Yeah, maybe," I said, returning his handshake with a blank stare. "Thanks again."

I watched him walk away then focused on the man who was heading down the ladder. When he reached the bottom rung, he turned around, and my mouth dropped open.

"Bob?"

"Hey," Robert Tompkins said, tossing the cattle prod on the ground. He took a quick look at the unconscious clowns, then walked toward us.

"What on earth are you doing here?" I said.

"I came to see the show," he said, shrugging. "But when I got here, I found out it had been canceled. Somebody killed the old man, huh?"

"Yeah, they did," I said, studying him closely. "But why are you still here?"

"I was hunting those two down," he said, nodding at the clowns. "You think they're dead?"

"No, I'm pretty sure they're still breathing," I said. "Why were you looking for them?"

"I was sitting at home last night after I finally got Bella settled down."

"How's she doing?"

"Not well," he whispered.

"I'm sorry to hear that."

"Yeah, it's sad," he said, exhaling audibly. "Anyway, I was sitting there thinking about Sammy when I remembered something she said in her last letter."

"Okay," I said, frowning.

"She was talking about wanting to come home if she could make it," he said.

"Yeah, I remember you saying that."

"Then she made a comment about how she was desperate to get away from these clowns. When I first read it, I thought she was just making a general reference about all the people who worked in the circus. Then I got the idea that she might have actually been specifically talking about those two. It looks like I was right."

"Smart," I said, nodding. "You're pretty good at this stuff."

"I was about to say the same thing to you," he said. "How did you figure it out?"

"The dog told us," I said, rubbing the beagle's head.

Bob frowned then shook his head.

"If you say so," he said. "Look, I really need to get going. I've got a long drive ahead of me, and I have to take Bella to the doctor first thing in the morning. Tell the cops if they need to talk to me about what I did, they know where to find me."

"And you're not going anywhere, right?" I said. "At least, not while she's still alive."

"No, I'm not."

"Okay, I'll explain everything to the Chief when he gets here. He'll need to speak with you at some point."

"I'm sure he's got my number," Bob said, extending his hand. "Thank you. Maybe it'll help her out a bit knowing that Sammy's killers were caught."

"I hope it does," I said. "Take care of yourself."

"I'll do my best," he said, then headed out through the back of the tent.

"That guy deserves a medal," Josie said.

"He certainly does," I said, glancing at the entrance where Chief Abrams was striding toward us.

He came to a stop in front of me then glanced around and spotted the two clowns who were slowly regaining consciousness. Then he noticed my forehead, the dirt in my hair, and the fact that I was only wearing one shoe.

"Sexy," he deadpanned. "You want to catch me up?"

I did.

When I finished, he placed a call to Detective Williams, then hung up and handcuffed the two clowns to each other. He walked back to us then glanced around the tent again deep in thought. I waited for questions as I petted the beagle who remained tucked under Josie's arm.

"The dog told you it was those two who threw them off the boat?" he said.

"She did," I said.

"Yup," Josie said, nodding.

"I really need to learn how to speak dog," he said. "And your escape plan was to climb that ladder?"

"Well, it really wasn't much of a plan," I said, shrugging. "It was more of an evasive maneuver."

"I imagine it was," he said. "Then you did a header off the platform into Miguel's arms."

"It wasn't as romantic as it sounds, Chief."

"Just a little more of that circus love, right?"

"There you go," I said, grinning. "I take it you haven't gotten a confession out of Claude yet."

"As a matter of fact, we haven't," he said. "But we will."

240

"No, you won't," I said, shaking my head.

"Because?" the Chief said, raising an eyebrow at me.

"Because he didn't do it," I said without emotion. "I wish he had, but he didn't."

"But you know who did?"

"Yeah, I think so," I said, tearing up.

"Are you going to tell me?"

"Eventually," I said. "I need to have a chat with somebody first."

"Suzy, don't start," he snapped.

"It's okay, Chief," I said. "Nobody's in any danger."

"That's really not your call, *young lady*."

"Good one, Chief," I said, laughing. "You've almost got it down."

"Who do you need to talk to?" he said.

"Wanda."

"The aerialist?"

"Yeah."

"Why the heck do you need to talk to her?" Chief Abrams said.

"Good question," Josie said.

"Thanks. I thought so too," the Chief said.

"I just need a quick word with her about her plans for the future," I said, glancing over at the two clowns who were struggling to sit up. "Has Freddie had a chance to take a look at the syringe you found in Claude's bag?"

"Actually, he has," the Chief said.

"Did he find any traces of what was in it?"

"He did," the Chief said, nodding. "And you'll never guess what it was."

"Insulin," I whispered, staring off into the distance. "I'll be back in a few minutes."

"How the heck did you know that?" the Chief called out.

I kept walking toward the curtains that led to the performer area.

"I suppose the dog told you that too?"

Chapter 27

I found Wanda in a small makeshift structure near the area where the animals were held. She was packing two suitcases and seemed to be in a hurry to get it done. She was surprised to see me but waved me inside.

"Hey," she said. "Miggy was just catching me up on what happened. Wow, that's a nasty crease you've got on your forehead. Are you okay?"

"Yeah, I'll be fine," I said.

"I hate to tell you, but I don't think I see a circus career in your future."

"I don't think Miguel would survive long trying to catch me," I said, managing a small laugh. "Where is he?"

"He's outside packing. We rented a truck today."

"You're driving to Vegas?" I said.

"We thought it would be fun," she said, brushing her hair back from her face. "Neither one of us has ever driven cross-country. At least on our own."

"Give yourself lots of time," I said. "It's quite a hike."

"We've got a week before we start the new job," she said, glancing around for other items to pack.

"I need to talk to you, Wanda," I said. "And it's a conversation I wish with all my heart that I didn't need to have."

"This sounds serious," she said, sitting down and gesturing for me to do the same.

"I couldn't help but notice that you're always checking with Miguel to make sure he's eaten," I said. "And asking him how he's doing."

"What about it?" Wanda said, frowning.

"At first, I thought it was cute the way you were looking after him," I said. "And it's obvious how much you guys mean to each other."

"We're brother and sister," she said, shrugging. "Isn't that what we're supposed to do?"

"Of course," I said. "But there's more to it, isn't there?"

"Take the marbles out of your mouth, Suzy," Wanda said, staring at me.

"Miguel's diabetic, isn't he?"

"As a matter of fact, he is," she said. "How on earth do you know that? He never talks about it."

"It came to me tonight when I hanging in mid-air and I saw the needle tracks on his arms. At first, I thought he might be a druggie, but he's not the type. He takes such good care of himself. And then I put two and two together."

"Two and two?" she said, confused. "I'm not following."

"Pontilly was killed by an injection behind the ear," I said.

"What?" she said, stunned. "Is that how Claude killed him? The cops wouldn't talk about what happened. I couldn't believe it when they handcuffed him and dragged him away earlier."

"Yeah, that's how he died," I said. "But Claude didn't kill him."

"What are you talking about?" Wanda said with a deep frown.

"The medical examiner found traces of insulin in the syringe."

"What?" Wanda said, shaking her head. Then she tried to recover and deflect. "Well, anybody could have done that. There's probably a lot of diabetics who work here."

"Yeah, you're probably right," I said. "But I doubt if any of them were being threatened by Pontilly and the clowns."

Wanda folded her hands in her lap and sat quietly.

"Pontilly was threatening you, wasn't he?"

Wanda managed a silent nod.

"He said if you left the circus, you were going to regret it," I said.

"He did," she whispered. "And he sent Bubs and Chuckles around a few times to rough me up a little. You know, just to get my attention."

"And you told Miguel what was going on?" I said.

"No, he overheard Pontilly and the clowns talking the other night about all the lovely things they'd like to do to us."

"Did you and Miguel talk about it?"

"We did," she said, tearing up. "But he told me not to worry about it. He said he'd take care of it."

"Because nobody messes with his sister, right?"

"Yeah, Miggy's good about things like that. I never have to worry when he's around," she said, then took a couple of deep breaths. "But I had no idea he'd ever do something like that. You really think he killed Mr. Pontilly?"

"I wish I didn't. But, yes, I do."

She sat quietly for a long time trying to process the fact that her brother had killed the old man.

"He's never been quite the same since that fall," she said. "But I can't believe he could do something like that."

"I'm sure he was just trying to protect you," I said.

"Yeah, I'm sure he was," she said, exhaling loudly. "So, what now?"

"You need to talk to Miguel and get your story together. Then you need to speak with the cops. Maybe they'll decide there were extenuating circumstances. After all, they were threatening you."

"Maybe he can claim self-defense," Wanda said, staring at me.

"A chiseled trapeze artist defending himself from a ninety-year-old man who barely weighed a hundred pounds?" I said, frowning. "I'm afraid you'll have to do better than that."

"Yeah, you're probably right," she said.

"Have to do better than what?" Miguel said, poking his head inside.

"Come on in, Miggy," Wanda said.

246

"Yeah, I need to get going," I said, giving him a hug on my way out. "Thanks again for catching me."

"No problem," he said, glancing nervously at his sister.

I headed for the animal area and walked past the two tigers who were asleep and snoring loudly. But the elephant was wide awake and immediately made eye contact with me as I approached. I came to a stop directly in front of her, and she raised her trunk and gently draped it over my shoulder. I stroked it and stared back at her.

"How would you like to get out of here and come home with us?"

The elephant raised her trunk into the air and let loose with a trumpet blast that probably woke half the town.

"I think she likes the idea," Josie said.

I turned around and noticed Queen B. wagging her tail as she stared up at the elephant.

"All creatures great and small, right?" I said, reaching out to pet the beagle.

"Yeah. Maybe our species will figure it out someday," Josie said.

"I have my doubts."

"You having a glass-half-empty kind of night?" she said.

"Yeah. Death and murder always depress me," I said. "You ready to get out of here?"

"I am," she said. "Let's drop Queen B. off then head home for a nightcap."

"Why don't you take off?" I said. "I need to have a chat with the Chief. I'll get a ride home with him."

"Okay," she said. "But I think you should have your head examined."

"No, crazy jokes tonight, okay? I'm not in the mood."

"I'm not talking about that, you idiot," she said, laughing. "I'm talking about having the doctor take a look at the dent in your forehead."

Chapter 28

I followed the Chief into the Clay Bay police station, a small granite building semi-covered in ivy that was located close to downtown. I glanced at the clock on the wall and immediately stifled a yawn when I realized it was almost one in the morning.

"I'll put a pot of coffee on," the Chief said.

"Coffee sounds great," I said.

"You won't be saying that after you taste it," he said with a grin. "At home, I'm not allowed within twenty feet of the coffeemaker."

"What do you think is going to happen to Miguel?" I said, putting my feet up on his desk.

"Hard to say," the Chief said. "He confessed without putting up a fight. And their story about how they felt their lives were in danger sounds plausible. But that doesn't change the fact that he's guilty of the premeditated murder of a ninety-year-old man. The prosecution is gonna have a field day with that."

"What did Miguel have to say about how it all went down?" I said, yawning and putting my hands behind my head.

"You really need to stop watching so many cop shows," he said, sitting down behind his desk. "I think Miguel's tongue wasn't the only thing he damaged when he missed the net in Colorado."

"Scrambled neurons?"

"I knew you'd understand," the Chief said with a big grin.

"Funny."

"He said he did it as payback for what Pontilly was thinking about doing to his sister."

"And he and Wanda were already suspicious that the old man was behind what happened to Samantha?"

"They were. He went into the wardrobe room when everybody was outside taking a break. Snuck up behind him and injected a full syringe of insulin behind his ear."

"And that drove Pontilly's blood sugars down, right?"

"Way down," the Chief said. "At some point, Pontilly would have slipped into a coma, then the overdose eventually finished him off."

"Nobody found him in the wardrobe room?"

"Apparently, Pontilly had a strict ritual before a show. And a big part of it was being left alone," the Chief said.

"Man, what a horrible way to die."

"Yeah, bad way to go out," the Chief said over the gurgle of the coffeemaker.

"You do know that you're going to have to hire a crew to take down the tents and figure out what to do with all the circus equipment," I said.

"I do," he said. "But it can wait."

"We're taking the elephant and the tigers," I said.

"Why am I not surprised?

"But just on a temporary basis," I said, glancing across the desk.

"Of course," he said with a smile. "Just a temporary thing."

The Chief's phone chirped, and he answered on the second ring.

"Chief Abrams...Hey, Williams...How about that? It's nice when they make it easy...Yeah, I get that. But that sounds like an insult to the box of rocks...Okay. I'll be back in the office sometime before noon. Thanks."

He ended the call and tossed his phone on the desk.

"Detective Williams, I presume," I said, yawning.

"He called from the ambulance. He's escorting the two clowns down to Upstate Medical. Apparently, they both need multiple surgeries."

"Good."

The Chief laughed as he headed for the coffeemaker and poured two cups.

"Just outside of Watertown, they started throwing each other under the bus."

"Did they happen to mention why they threw her off the boat?"

"Detective Williams said they were babbling about how she was threatening to go public and take the circus down. It sounds like they were definitely acting on Pontilly's instructions."

"I just can't figure out why she would all of a sudden start doing that," I said. "She'd worked there for years."

"Haven't you figured out enough stuff for one night?" he said, handing me a cup.

"Yeah, I should probably quit while I'm ahead. It sure smells good."

I took a sip then grimaced.

"How is it?" the Chief said, taking a sip.

"It sure smells good."

"I warned you," he said. "After we drink these, we'll head back to the cells and turn Master Claude loose."

"Let him wait," I said, forcing another sip down. "You know, you might want to try adding water to the coffee grounds."

"Too strong?"

"Not if you like drinking road tar."

We finished our coffee, then I followed the Chief through the door that led to two small cells in the back of the station. The cells would never be mistaken for a maximum-security facility, but the bars were solid, and the doors locked tight. Claude sat up on his cot when we entered.

"What are you doing here?" he said, glaring at me.

"Unfortunately, I'm here to keep you from going to prison."

"Really?" he grunted.

"But now that I see you in a cage, I kind of like it," I said. "It works for you."

"What's she talking about?" Claude said to the Chief.

"Suzy thinks she might know who killed Pontilly," the Chief said, delivering his line perfectly.

"Well, that's great. I told you somebody put that syringe in my bag," Claude said, turning to me. "Who was it?"

"My memory is a little fuzzy at the moment," I said.

"Considering the crease in your forehead, I'm not surprised," Claude said, laughing. "What did you do?"

"Trapeze accident," I said, gently pressing the bruise on my forehead and realizing that it was, in fact, slightly indented. "Weird," I said with a frown.

"You'll get no argument from me," Claude said.

"You know, I think I changed my mind, Chief," I said, wheeling around. "Let's just let him rot in here."

"Hang on," Claude said. "I was just kidding. Are you gonna tell me who killed the old man or not?"

"Maybe," I said. "But first, you have to agree to one thing."

"Like what?" Claude said, his eyes narrowing.

"You need to agree to turn over the tigers and the elephant to me," I said.

"Why would I do that?"

"Because I said so," I said, putting my hands on my hips. "You are officially out of the animal act business." Then I smiled at him. "But maybe you can make a comeback as a clown. They're down a couple at the moment."

"What are you gonna do with them?" Claude said.

"Apart from making their lives as comfortable as possible, not a thing," I said.

Claude thought about it for a few moments, then shrugged.

"Okay. Why not?" he said. "Actually, you'll be doing me a favor."

"Don't remind me," I said.

"So, who killed Mr. Pontilly?"

"Miguel," the Chief said.

"The Silent One killed the old man?" Claude said. "Why the heck did he do that?"

"He had his reasons," the Chief said.

"Can I get out of here now? I need to get back to the circus and check in with everybody. We have to figure out what we're going to do now that Pontilly's gone. But without the animal acts and the aerialists, it's gonna be tough sledding for a while."

"Yeah, that's what they thought," I said.

"What are you talking about?" he said, confused.

"They all left earlier tonight on the boat," I said.

"What?"

"Yeah, they all bailed. I guess they figured the *world-famous* Pontilly Family Circus had finally run its course."

"I can't believe they left without me," he said.

"Yeah, they were heartbroken to leave you behind," I deadpanned. "But I imagine they were sure you were going away for a long time."

"I'll explain everything when I track them down," he said. "Did they say where they were going?"

"Actually, they did. I think I've got it written down somewhere," I said, digging into my pocket for a slip of paper. "Yeah, here it is. But I can't read the handwriting."

"Let me see it," Claude said, approaching the bars.

I handed the slip of paper to him, and he peered down at it.

"That's horrible penmanship," he said. "Is that a J or an I?"

He continued to stare down at the slip of paper trying to decipher what I'd scribbled a few minutes ago at Chief Abrams' desk. Then I wound up and fired the best punch I'd ever thrown between the bars. It landed with a crack, and Claude tumbled backward holding his nose that was already gushing blood.

"Good punch," the Chief said.

"Thanks," I said, rubbing my hand. "But I hurt my hand."

"I'd be surprised if you didn't," he said. "Man, you're falling apart tonight. We better get you home before you do any more damage to yourself."

"What about him?" I said, nodding at Claude who was staring at his hands that were covered in blood.

"He can wait awhile," the Chief said. "Besides, he's already missed his ride."

We headed for the door but stopped when Claude yelled.

"Hey. You can't do that," Claude said.

"Do what?" the Chief said.

"Hit me like that," he said. "That's police brutality."

"Normally, I'd agree with you, Claude," the Chief said. "But not this time."

"Why the hell not?"

The Chief gave the bleeding man with the broken nose a big grin.

"Because she's not a cop."

Chapter 29

I watched Josie climb the stepladder to inspect the back of the elephant's ears. The elephant continued using her trunk to toss copious amounts of hay and fruit into her mouth and didn't bat an eye as Josie continued the exam. She climbed down and put the ladder away before joining me.

"How's she doing?" I said.

"Apart from some scarring, the last vestiges of the bullhook are gone forever," she said, patting the elephant's trunk.

"She seems happy here," I said.

"As much as I hate to admit it, she does," Josie said.

"Does that mean you want to keep her?"

"No, it does not," she said, gently punching me on the shoulder. "I merely said she seems happy."

"I'm not sure we're going to be able to find a good place for her to go," I said.

"You found a home for the tigers in two days," Josie said.

"Yeah, we got lucky with that," I said, deflecting. "Who knew there was a tiger reserve in Texas?"

"She needs room to roam, Suzy."

"I know," I said, then pointed out at the acreage. "But I thought that when we finish the fence around the perimeter, we could also add another fence inside that. We could run it off the caged area a couple hundred yards in from the perimeter fence and take it all around the property. By the time we were done, Beulah would have several acres to wander around on."

"She should have a lot more room than that," Josie said.

"In a perfect world, yes," I said, firmly. "But she's been in captivity since she was a baby. She wouldn't have a clue about how to survive in the wild."

"I'm not talking about releasing her into the wild."

"And if we sent her to a reserve, who knows if the other elephants there would accept her? And what about poachers?"

"Suzy."

"We just need to take our time and make sure we find the perfect spot for her."

"Unless you're able to build her the perfect spot right here first?"

"Maybe," I said with a shrug. "Just look at her. She loves it here."

"Unbelievable," Josie said, shaking her head. Then she stared off into the distance and laughed. "Here comes the floorshow."

I followed her eyes and saw Jill coming through the gate off the back of the dog's play area. She closed the gate behind her, then placed Queen B. on the ground. The beagle raced across the field, making a beeline for us. Beulah spotted her and trumpeted then placed the tip of her trunk on the ground. The beagle slowed but didn't stop, and she scooted up the trunk, climbed to the top, then perched herself on the elephant's back and began surveying the scene. Then she nuzzled one of Beulah's ears.

"Besides, Queen B. would never forgive us if we sent Beulah away," I said, making a face at Josie.

"I repeat; unbelievable," Josie said.

"Your three o'clock is here," Jill said to Josie. "And your mother wants to have a chat with you."

"Did she call?" I said.

"No, she's waiting in your office," Jill said, laughing. "With the binder."

"Okay," I said, shrugging. "Another round of wedding dress debate."

"Let's get going," Josie said. "I'm not looking forward to this one. Audrey is bringing her Chihuahua in for his shots."

"Ew," I said, frowning. "Billy the Biter?"

"Yeah, he got me good last year."

"You want to trade?" I said. "I'll swap you my mother for the dog straight up."

"Not a chance," Josie said, then glanced at Jill. "You coming?"

"No, I thought I'd stay here for a while," she said. "I love watching these two playing together."

"Have fun," I said, waving as we headed across the field.

My mother was sitting on the couch studying the binder when I entered my office. I gave her a hug and a kiss on the cheek before I sat down behind my desk. I grabbed a bag of bite-sized from the drawer, ignored the disapproving look she was giving me, and popped one of the morsels.

"I suppose I could ask the dressmaker to use Velcro," my mother said. "You know, so it's adjustable."

"Funny, Mom. Are you here for a reason, or did you just stop by to harass me?"

"Harsh, darling," she said, laughing. "Actually, I just wanted to give you an update on the photographer and videographer."

"So, 60 Minutes turned you down?"

"You're on fire today, darling," she said, raising an eyebrow at me. "Since Max is back in town, I would have thought you'd have taken the edge off by now."

"My edges are none of your business, Mom," I said. "Would you like to stay for dinner?"

"That sounds wonderful," she said. "Who's cooking?"

"Chef Claire."

"You're making her cook on her night off? No wonder she feels like she needs a break."

"She insisted," I said. "She's testing out a new recipe that she says is *positively exotic.*"

"Then I'm definitely staying for dinner," she said. "You'll be pleased to know I've finally found the perfect wedding dress for you. And matching bridesmaids' dresses as well."

"Thank you," I said, glancing up at the ceiling.

"You're welcome."

"I wasn't talking to you, Mom."

"And I have an idea for entertainment," she said. "But I need to run it by you first."

"As long as it's not a circus, I'm sure it'll be fine. What are you thinking of?"

"I thought we should have some nice piano music at some point in the evening," she said, choosing her words carefully.

"Sure," I said, popping another bite-sized. "That sounds great."

"But later on, people will probably want to dance," she said, casually.

"It's been known to happen at weddings," I said. "I'm sure there's a ton of wedding bands working around here."

"Wedding band," she said, scoffing. "Right. Like that's going to happen."

"Get to the point, Mom," I said.

"I was thinking about hiring a popular band that everyone has heard of," she said.

"Which one?" I said, cocking my head at her.

"L.E.N.," she said, tossing it out for me to process.

"Summerman's band?"

"Well, actually, I think it's more his nephew's band than Summerman's these days. But, yes, that's the one I'm thinking of."

"A couple of issues do come to mind, Mom."

"I'm sure they do, darling."

"First of all, they're one of the hottest bands on the planet, and I don't think they get near a stage for less than half a million bucks these days."

"It's seven hundred thousand, actually."

"Well, there you go. There is no way you are going to pay *anybody* seven hundred grand to play at my wedding," I said, glaring at her. "End of discussion."

"Of course not," she said. "Do I look like an idiot? But Summerman has been kind enough to offer to do it for a considerable discount."

"How much of a discount?"

"He's offered to do it for free as a wedding gift," she said.

"What?"

"It's an incredibly generous offer," she said.

"You got that right. I would have been happy with an autographed CD," I said, baffled.

"Do you think Josie will be okay with it?"

"I have no idea," I said, remembering how badly her brief but intense relationship with the musician had ended. "You didn't agree yet, did you?"

"No, I told Summerman that I would have to discuss it with you and Josie."

"Thanks, Mom," I said. "So, he's around?"

"He was," my mother said. "But he said he had to head off somewhere for the next few weeks. But he wouldn't tell me where. He's so mysterious at times."

"Yeah, mysterious. That's the word for it," I said.

Epilogue

I closed my book and set it on the nightstand, then snuggled close to Max who was making short work of the Patricia Highsmith mystery I'd recommended. I glanced at the clock, decided that six in the morning on a Saturday was way too early to get out of bed and closed my eyes.

"I saw the Hitchcock movie, but I can't believe I never read the book," Max said, draping an arm over my shoulders. "It's great."

"I know."

"This guy Bruno is a total psychopath," he said.

"Yup."

"Reading about a train ride has got me thinking," Max said. "We should take a train trip sometime. Maybe the one that goes up the Pacific coast."

"That sounds like fun," I said, yawning.

"You going back to sleep for a while?"

"I thought I might," I said, draping a leg over his.

"Take a nap," he said. "Then I'll make you breakfast."

"Pancakes?" I said, opening one eye.

"Whatever you want," he said, gently squeezing my shoulder. "Yeah, a train trip sounds good. I wonder how much the tickets are."

Completely at peace, I dozed off and dreamt of trains. And train movies. Then movies in general. Eventually, I found myself standing outside the entrance to a movie I desperately wanted to see, but I couldn't find my ticket. And a man wearing a canary yellow tuxedo was blocking the door telling me that I couldn't watch the movie without a ticket. No ticket, no movie he repeated over and over. I was just about to poke the guy with my cattle prod when I woke with a start and sat up in bed.

"Please, don't do that," Max said, clutching his chest with one hand as he reached for the book he'd dropped with the other.

"Sorry," I said, patting his arm as I stared at the wall.

"What on earth is the matter?"

"He bought the tickets."

"What?"

"He bought the tickets."

"I'm marrying a crazy woman," Max said, laughing. "Who bought what tickets?"

I climbed out of bed and did my best to explain my thinking as I got dressed.

"And you're just going to drive there this morning?" he said, tossing his book on the bed.

"Yes."

"You want me to tag along?"

"No, I think I need to do this by myself."

"Maybe you should take the Chief with you," he said, getting out of bed.

"No, he's fishing today," I said. "I can't ruin his day off again."

"Well, at least call him from the road," Max said.

"That I can do. Where are you going?"

"To make coffee," he said, pulling on his robe. "I'll fix you a traveler."

"Aren't you sweet," I said, giving him a quick hug and a kiss.

Fifteen minutes later, I was in my SUV and doing my best to fend off the early morning glare. I called the Chief and set my phone in its dashboard holder.

"Good morning," the Chief said.

"Are you already on the River?"

"I am," he said. "And I just finished doing battle with what must have been a ten pound Northern."

"But you lost him?"

"Sadly, yes," he said. "What's up?"

I spent a few minutes telling him where I was going. He waited until I finished, then turned fatherly.

"Why are you doing this, Suzy?"

"You know the answer to that question."

"Yeah, closure. I get it," he said. "But I don't think it's a good idea. What happens if he gets scared and decides to do something stupid?"

"He won't."

"Because?" the Chief said.

"Because he's no threat. And I'm going to convince him I understand what he's been going through."

"If you want to wait an hour, I'll go with you."

"No, you just enjoy your day," I said.

"At least make sure he knows that people know where you are."

"I will."

"Call me when you're done. And please be careful."

"Will do. Later."

I ended the call and focused on the road as I began formulating the set of questions I needed answered. I turned up the volume on the Keith Jarrett CD the Chief had given me, and his intricate piano work produced a touch of melancholy that seemed appropriate. An hour later, I saw the red truck in the driveway and pulled in behind it. I climbed the short set of steps that led to the front porch and knocked softly. Moments later, he opened the door and stared in disbelief.

"Suzy," Bob Tompkins said. "What are you doing here?"

"I need to talk to you," I said.

"Sure," he said with a shrug and waved me inside the house. "Have a seat. You want something to drink?"

"No, thanks, I'm good," I said, sitting down in an overstuffed chair.

He sat down across from me and draped a leg over his knee.

"How's Bella doing?" I said.

"I'm afraid I'm going to have to put her in an assisted living facility soon. A couple of nights ago, she had something on the stove, forgot about it, and almost burned her place down."

"I'm sorry to hear that," I said.

"She'll be better off there. And I'll visit her every day. But she's slipping fast," Bob said through a wave of emotion. "For now, she still remembers who I am."

"That's so sad," I said, feeling completely useless as I always did when offering condolences to the grieving.

"Yes, it is," Bob said, then switched to a less painful topic. "I've been following what's happening with the two clowns. The cops have been pretty good about keeping me in the loop."

"I heard they're out of the hospital," I said.

"They are," he said, nodding. "It looks like they're only going to be charged with manslaughter."

"That sucks," I said. "Miguel is being charged with murder."

"How do they decide who gets charged with what?" he said, frowning. "It seems very arbitrary at times."

"Leave it to the lawyers, right?" I said, shrugging.

"What happened to his sister?"

"She's working in Vegas and trying to figure out how to pay his legal bills."

"Have you heard anything else?" he said.

"Apparently, the old man was in serious debt."

"And he couldn't afford to have Sammy walking around saying bad things about the circus or making threats," Bob said.

"That seems to be the reason he had the clowns throw her off the boat," I said.

"I wish I'd gotten a chance to have a little chat with him," Bob said. "Did the people working at the circus really just head off and leave everything behind?"

"They did. Fortunately, several of Pontilly's creditors showed up and hauled most of it away. Except for the elephant. We took her."

"You kept the elephant?" he said, frowning at me.

"Yeah," I said with a grin. "She's great."

"I'll take your word for it," he said, chuckling. "Okay, I'm sure you didn't come all this way for a social chat. What's up?"

"I'd like to ask you about the night Samantha's dad killed himself," I said.

"What about it?" Bob said, confused.

"This is going to sound incredibly insensitive on my part," I said, staring at him.

"Forewarned is forearmed?" he said, now even more confused.

"Yeah, let's hope so."

"Go ahead," he said, leaning forward.

"Nobody was too broken up when they heard he killed himself, right? Including you."

He visibly flinched, then sat back in his chair and stared at me.

"Why on earth would you ask me that question?"

"Insensitive, huh?" I said. "I warned you."

"Next time I'll believe you," he said, shaking his head.

"But nobody really grieved over his death, did they?"

"No, they didn't," he said after a long pause. "He was a deplorable human being who treated Bella and Samantha horribly. And he was universally disliked by pretty much everyone he came in contact with."

"Was he abusive to Bella and Samantha?"

"He was. Especially when he'd been drinking," Bob said, staring off as the memories returned. "And he drank constantly."

"It must have been a terrible situation for them," I said.

"The worst," he said. "If Bella had been a bit more stable, they could have gotten out. I even offered to help them, but Bella was convinced she wasn't strong enough to handle it on her own."

"So, she decided to stay and just take it?"

"She did," Bob said, exhaling audibly. "Even after she saw what was happening to Sammy, she still refused to leave."

"What was happening to her?"

"She was turning into her mother," he said. "And the more abusive he got, the more identical they became. It was like they'd made some sort of unspoken pact to show him exactly what he'd done to them. And when Sammy started doing that thing with her head, I freaked out. She scared the hell out of me."

"You were having an affair with Bella, weren't you?"

He flinched again and stared off into the distance for a long time. I waited it out, and he eventually made eye contact and slowly nodded his head.

"Yes," he whispered. "But it was a lot more than that."

"I can see that," I said. "You've spent the last thirty years taking care of her."

"I'd do anything for Bella."

"I'm sure you would," I said, nodding.

I stared at him then tossed it out with a whisper.

"Even kill her husband, right?"

He gave me a wild-eyed stare as he gripped the armrests with both hands.

"What?"

"Samantha and her mother were at the movies the night he died," I said.

"What about it?"

"It was your idea for them to go to the movies that night, wasn't it? You even bought the tickets for them."

"How could you possibly know that?" he said, stunned.

"To tell you the truth, Bob, I have no idea where that one came from," I said with a shrug. "But I'm right, aren't I?"

"Yes," he whispered.

"And after they left the house, you went over to see him."

"I did," he said, staring at me. "My plan was to confront him. I figured if Bella wouldn't leave, maybe I could convince him to go. With him gone, I thought she and Sammy would have a chance."

"Was he drunk when you got there?" I said.

"He was already passed out in his chair," he said, the words coming easier now. "I stood over him and watched that sorry excuse for a husband and father snore and drool for several minutes. Then the idea just came to me."

"You carried him out to his car, splashed some scotch around, then left him in the garage with the engine running and the door closed," I said. "Then you went home."

"Then I went home," he whispered.

Then he broke down and began sobbing. Maybe after thirty years of silence and keeping his secret buried in the catacombs, he would feel better getting it off his chest and sharing it with someone. But he certainly wasn't feeling better at the moment. I waited patiently for him to finish as a wave of sympathy for him washed over me.

And Samantha.

But most of all, I felt sorry for Bella.

He took a couple of deep breaths then wiped his eyes with his sleeve.

"Wow," he said. "I can't believe you got that out of me."

"It wasn't my intention to hurt you, Bob," I whispered. "I'm very sorry."

"I hope you'll explain your intentions at some point."

"I'll give it a shot," I said with a small shrug. "You thought if you got him out of the way, the three of you might be able to build a life together."

"Yeah, that was *my* craziness making itself known," he said.

"But you never got a chance to see if it would work," I said. "Right after her dad died, Samantha ran off, and her mom's problems started getting worse."

"Pretty much. At first, Bella seemed a bit better, but it didn't last long."

"Did Samantha know about you and her mom?"

"I think she had her suspicions, but we never talked about it," he said. "I was going to tell her as soon as she made her way home."

"Bella doesn't know what really happened that night, does she?"

"No," he whispered down to the floor. "How did you know that?"

"It was the way she was talking to her dead husband the day the Chief and I were at her house," I said. "She kept calling him a coward. Actually, it was more of a chant."

"Yeah, I've heard that particular rant hundreds of times," he said, then fixed a hard stare on me. "Bella can never know."

"Okay," I said, nodding. "Do you ever wonder if things might have turned out differently if you'd told her what you did?"

"Only about a dozen times a day," he said with a sad smile.

"Sure, I get that," I said. "So, you stuck around here all this time just to take care of her?"

"I did. I asked her a couple of times to marry me or at least agree to live together, but she wouldn't have it," he said. "I think she thought that was *her* best way to take care of *me*. You know, not letting herself get that close to anybody ever again given what was happening to her. If that makes any sense."

"As much sense as anything else," I said with a shrug. "You stuck around all these years out of love and guilt?"

"I guess when you boil it all down, that pretty much sums it up," he said. "Quite a life I've carved out for myself, huh?"

"I think what you did is noble, Bob," I said, then frowned. "I mean, taking care of Bella, not the murder thing."

"What are you going to do now?" he said, again leaning forward in his chair.

"Is that your way of asking me if I'm going to tell the cops?"

"The thought did cross my mind," he said, studying me closely.

"If I was going to do that, Bob, I would have brought the cops with me."

"So, you're not going to tell anybody?"

"And take away Bella's last connection to the real world? No, I don't think I can do that."

"Thank you."

274

"I'm not doing it for you, Bob. If it all came out now and you went to prison, it would probably kill her faster than a hose filled with carbon monoxide. And from what I see, you've already been in your own prison for the past thirty years.

"I suppose I have," he said, then frowned. "Let me get this straight, you came all the way out here just to confirm your suspicions?"

"Pretty much," I said, shrugging. "And it would have kept me up at night."

"Do you have any idea how strange that sounds?"

"Yeah, I really need to start working on that."

"Based on my own personal experience trying to change the weird, I don't like your chances."

For some reason, I found his comment funny, and I laughed long and hard. Then I wished him and Bella good luck and said my goodbyes. A few minutes after I hit the highway, I called the Chief.

"Hey," he said. "I just caught a beautiful Northern that had to be fifteen pounds."

"And you let it go, right?"

"I did," he said, laughing. "You've finally shamed me into catch and release."

"It took you long enough," I said, laughing along.

"How did it go with Tompkins?"

I stared out at the road and thought about prisons, both the physical kind designed to confine as well as the ones we create for ourselves.

I thought about Bella and Samantha and the prisons they'd found themselves locked in by the powerful combination of genetics and fate then contemplated the parallels with abused wild animals trapped in small cages, also imprisoned through no fault of their own.

I thought about Bob and knew for a fact that no brick and mortar facility could ever match the one he'd built for himself and continued to live in to this day.

Then for some reason, I thought about the Queens Beagle perched on top of the elephant's back.

When the image of the beagle quizzically surveying the world from a great height registered as a manifestation of the freedom to explore, I thought about Chef Claire and her relentless desire to learn and grow in the hope of realizing her full potential.

And for the second time today, I felt completely at peace.

"Are you still there?" the Chief said.

"Yeah, sorry about that," I said, deciding to tell him a small lie. "There was a deer next to the side of the road, and I wanted to make sure she was safe."

"I'd expect nothing less," he said. "So, how did it go with Tompkins?"

"My theory was a total washout," I said, feeling both good and bad about lying to one of my best friends. "I totally whiffed on that one."

"Well, you can't be right all the time," he said. "Besides, it's ancient history."

"Yeah," I whispered. "For some people."

"What?"

"Nothing. You feel like meeting for lunch?"

"Sounds great," the Chief said. "C.'s?"

"Of course."

"Do you know what the special is today?"

"No. But I hope it's one of the new dishes she's been working on. I think I'm in the mood for something exotic."

"Nice to see you embracing change," the Chief said, laughing.

"Baby steps, right?"

"Exactly."

"I'll see you there, Chief."

I ended the call and turned the music up. I glanced at myself in the rear-view mirror then shrugged.

"Or maybe I'll just go with a burger."